MARISSA ALMA NICK

REBEL

IN

VENUS

A NOVEL

Rebel In Venus © 2023

Manufactured and printed in the United States of America by BookBaby.

Support by Pioneer Winter Collective and Alma Dance Theater

Editing by Armando J. Bedenbaugh-Cortes and Marissa Alma Nick

Mentorship by Miguel Hernandez, Amliv Sotomayor, Mary Luft, Naima Ramos-Chapman, Nancy Nick, Henry Nick, Katiana Marchena

The Library of Congress has established a Cataloging-in-Publication record for this title.

Print ISBN: 978-1-66789-263-4 | eBook ISBN: 978-1-66789-264-1

FIRST LARGE PRINT EDITION

Printed in the United States of America

10 9

This Large Print edition published in accord with the standards of the N.A.V.H

TRIGGER WARNING:

REBEL IN VENUS contains scenes, details, and situations that trigger PTSD and emotional trauma. Scenes of sex, drugs, abuse, rape, and suicide, may cause discomfort to some readers. Please consider your own sensitivity beforehand.

For the girls, and anyone else daring to live a life free of shame.

TABLE OF CONTENTS

I'LL NEVER TELL

1

Maria lights up the half-smoked joint, passes it to me, and tells me about her ex-boyfriend, Scott.

Me: You mean the douche actor man-boy with three cars, two condos and an Emmy? That fucking Scott!

Maria: Yeah! The one who used to rape me in my sleep! And you know!...I never even knew it was happening. Not until the day I checked my fucking nanny-cam...to try and find my car keys, and there he was, that shitty actor, fucking me in my sleep! And! On top of it... my baby girl was laying right next to us, in her crib!

I don't respond.

Maria: Hey Layla! Are you there? Layla hello!

Me: Yeah! Sorry.

Maria: Were you even listening to me?

Me: Yeah I was... I was.

Maria: It's fucked up, right?

I don't say anything.

Maria: Layla!

Me: Yes! Sorry! Sorry, yes. Yes it's really shitty, and totally fucked up. But you know... it's not that surprising. Honestly... it made me think of Andrew, that guy I dated after David, he actually did the same thing to me.

Maria: Really?! Andrew? And how'd you even find out?

Me: I'd wake up to it.

Maria: Gross.

Me: Honestly, I just tried to forget anything like that ever happened...like ever.

Maria: And how's that working out for you Layla?

Me: Well Maria, I'm totally fucked.

I take a hit, and a moment of silence.

Me: Especially because I feel like...

I exhale.

Me: Lately it's all coming up for me, and ...it feels like there's absolutely nothing I can do to stop it.

REBEL

IN

VENUS

MY FIRST DICK-PIC

2

It was a weekday, a Wednesday I think, and some time around noon. There wasn't a cloud in the sky, the air was humid, and the heat was thick.

It's so hot.

As I walked home from my friend Frida Perez's house, I feverishly sang Mariah Carey's "Always Be My Baby."

Cause you'll always be my...

At the time, Frida and I both lived in this little town, about fifteen minutes north of South Beach. It was very pedestrian friendly, the streets were lined with palm trees, and it was far away from all the clubs, and tourists. People walked, or rode their bikes often. There were a lot of families, an A-rated public elementary school, local restaurants, and best of all... direct access to the beach.

The sheer beauty of living on the beach is blinding.

While I walked home from Frida's that day, singing and feeling innocently blissful, I heard a car engine approaching from behind.

Am I in their way?

I looked back to see a very pale man, driving a very old brown car.

Do I know him?

I've seen that car.

So I walked further to the right.

Now I'm totally out of his way.

Then the pale man, who looked sort of familiar, yelled out to me:

"Look!"

And without hesitation, I looked.

Be careful, you might never forget what you saw.

What is that?

There it was, his oddly shaped, pale-pink penis, held in his large hand, and wearing the strangest smile on his face. He looked so proud of himself too... audaciously proud.

I don't even, I mean... what is that?!

Then he laughed.

I know that laugh.

At once, it was both comforting, and disturbing to know exactly who he was.

That's Frida's neighbor!

It was the same demented laugh Frida and I would hear, cackling from the other side of her backyard.

I hate that laugh.

I heard that exact laugh, while he held his pale-pink penis, and stared right into my dark brown eyes.

Why is he doing that?

Then he just drove off.

Where is he going?

He drove ferociously for two blocks, before parking his car... right next to Frida's house.

What was that?

My mind couldn't handle the terrifying shock of what had been forced onto me, so I quickly erased my memory by filling my mind with Maria Carey's hit single, and running all the way home.

Cause you'll always be my...

... does he know where I live?

* *

It was a weekday, a Wednesday I think...I remember I learned how to write in cursive that day, at school.

I feel so grown up.

That day, I got my very first, most unforgettable dick-pic, from a man we all knew as Mr. Jones, Miranda's dad.

His laugh.

His eyes.

His...

Why did he do that, to me?

I was seven years old.

Should I tell Miranda?

So were Frida, and Miranda.

HAIKU FOR A PEDOPHILE

3

Maria: That's fucked up Layla.

Me: Yeah it was.

I laugh uncomfortably.

Me: Honestly, I didn't even think you were listening to me, because of whatever you were doodling over there.

Maria: Oh no! Unlike you, I was listening! But I also wrote a haiku while listening to you.

Me: Oh, you did, did you?

Maria: I did! Do you want to hear it? I think you'll like it. It was inspired by your little dick-pic story.

Me: Sure, why not? What's it called?

I grab the joint from Maria's hand, and inhale.

Maria: "Haiku For A Pedophile."

I laugh so hard, I spit the joint right out of my mouth.

Me: What the fuck Maria?

We laugh.

Maria: Wait you gotta hear it, to really appreciate it.

Me: I'm sure.

Maria takes a good hit before beginning. Then she stands up, passes the joint back to me, and holds up the piece of paper she had been scribbling on.

Maria: Okay... eh-hem... "I want to love you. But you are too young for me. Don't care, I still will."

I laugh even harder.

Me: Maria no!... like...no! No Puedo!

Maria giggles, and takes a hit.

Maria: It's a little funny.

She passes me the joint, I take a hit, and pass it back.

Me: Yeah, it's almost as funny as the first time I ever masturbated...with a toy that looked like a ladybug.

Maria laughs as hard as I did at her pedophile haiku, and just like me, spits out the joint from her laughter.

Maria: Layla! Explain yourself!

A GOOD LUCK
NECK MASSAGE

4

When I was eight, my grandmother had this battery-operated neck massager, shaped like a giant ladybug. She won the toy-like prize in a highly competitive game night, better known as Friday Night Poker.

I love Friday's.

Things like bottle openers in the shape of alligators, or neck massagers disguised as ladybugs, were at great stake during these games.

Yes! Grandma won the cool ladybug thing!

The little massager my grandmother had won (which to me looked like a toy), would flutter, and vibrate whenever you clicked its little wings. But, unlike my toys that were kept in my toy-chest, the ladybug was tucked away in my grandmother's card drawer, and it would remain there all week long. That is, until Friday Night Poker at her friends, Claire and Eddies, where the ladybug would emerge. In fact, it had become a Friday night ritual for all the players, something all the adults called a "good luck neck massage."

* *

After poker, I'd often spend the night at my grandmother's, and while she would sleep in the next morning, I'd go quietly into the living room (which was frozen in time, circa-1977), and watch my favorite cartoons all by myself.

We're zany to the…

It was on one of those perfect all-to-myself mornings (while in the living room), that I decided to sneak into my grandmother's card drawer, and get the ladybug. I simply wanted to play with it, as I watched back-to-back episodes of Animaniacs; and figure out, once and for all, what the big deal was.

I wonder why everyone likes it.

My childlike mind was only searching for pleasure.

I grabbed the ladybug, sat down on the soft teal-colored carpet, turned on the ladybug, and put it on my neck… just like all the adults had done at poker.

That does feel really good.

But soon I began to wonder what it would feel like on the other parts of my body, too. So I tried it out… on my forearm, my elbow… even my stomach, calf, and quad. Then finally, I innocently made my way toward my inner thigh.

Whoa!

* *

It was official. I had done it. For the first time in my life, while watching cartoons, in my grandmother's 1977-esque living room, with the ladybug-toy she had won at poker… I had masturbated.

That feels good!

I remember I could not stop.

Again.

Again!!

Again!!!

Over and over, until the batteries died, and the ladybug's wings stopped flapping, I just kept on going.

Wow!

It was such an intuitive exploration, too.

Wait a minute.

There was however, something else that was as intuitive as discovering my own pleasure.

This is… bad.

Right?

It was a fear that I'd done something wrong, and I'd get in trouble if I were to get caught doing it.

I don't think I should be doing this.

But why not?

MIXED UP

5

I take a hit of the joint, and pass it to Maria.

Maria: So you masturbated when you were eight?

Me: Yeah, but I felt super guilty about it.

Maria: Shit, you know my cousin, she was twenty-two when she first masturbated, because my tia sex-shamed her at home. Poor thing actually thought if she touched herself, or had sex before she was married, the devil would snatch her coochi in her sleep!

We both laugh.

Maria: Damn! Is everything fucked up for little girls?

We stop laughing, and sit quietly for a few minutes.

Me: Well… so right after that, Eddie happened. And it became this sort of strange, and new sensation of physical pleasure, mixed with physical pain, and fear. But I didn't talk about it, or get it. I don't know, it was such a fucked-up swing of experiences. It's still not really too clear yet. It's all still… kinda cloudy, and pink.

NO PINK BALLOONS AT
MY BIRTHDAY PARTY

6

The walls were pink like pepto-bismol, and everything in the room was too.

Everything.

The shag carpet, curtains, wicker furniture, and bed set... all the same disgusting shade of pink.

I hate this place.

My eyes opened, and peered around the monochrome room, which looked a lot like the nightmare that had kept me up all night.

I don't think I slept.

I could smell coffee coming from the kitchen, which was mixing with the thick scent of Marlboro-lights.

I hate that smell.

Then, I felt someone behind me.

Who is that?

* *

The night before had been like every other Friday night.

Something feels wrong.

All the adults would play poker at Claire and Eddie's (Emily's grandparent's), while Emily and I would play with all of her toys, in the den. Accept on this Friday, I ended up sleeping over because it was my birthday weekend; and when it came time for bed, Emily was put in her bedroom... and I was taken to the guest room.

The pink room.

My dreams blur with reality, and my realities replay in my nightmares.

* *

Is this real?

I laid still, and wondered who was behind me.

Emily?

I thought maybe she'd had a nightmare like mine, and came to be with me because she was frightened. But the idea of it being Emily faded quickly, once I realized the overwhelming scale of the oversized hand, wrapped around my tiny frame.

I can't move.

It was even more obvious, once I smelled the alcohol.

Emily doesn't smell like that.

Emily doesn't hold me like that.

When did he get here?

Why is he lying there, like that, behind me?

Then he began to snore.

I hate that sound.

His snoring quickly grew louder, while his lifeless hand shifted down my trembling stomach, and his giant belly poked me in my back.

I could feel other parts of him too.

I have to get up.

The moment his grip loosened, I jumped out of the bed, and stood beside him.

Get up!

I stared at him, unable to move, with questions running through my confused mind.

When did you get here?

He laid there, in a deep sleep, wearing a large white tank top with a tattered left sleeve, and loose fitted white underwear.

He looks so dirty.

I looked around the pink room one more time.

Why is everything pink?

Every single corner, pink.

I hate pink.

I looked back at him, and moved close enough to have to smell him one more time. Cigarettes, and whiskey… a scent that would continue to leave me nauseous, even as an adult.

The imprint of you on my senses, makes me want to vomit.

What happened?

Suddenly, Claire walked in, and I stood, paralyzed next to Eddie (who was still laying in the bed, fast asleep).

What did I do?

I felt like I had been caught.

What for?

Teaching by way of shame is very effective.

Claire: Eddie?… Eddie get up!

But Eddie didn't move.

Claire: Layla! What are you doing?

I didn't say anything.

I don't know what to say.

Why is she screaming at me?

Claire shouted with more frustration.

Claire: Eddie! Eddie wake up!

But Eddie wasn't waking up, which made Claire angrier.

Is Emily okay?

Me: Where is Emily?

Claire: She's still asleep Layla!

Me: Oh.

I still wasn't sure if I could believe Claire.

She smells just like him.

Claire was emitting the same nauseating fragrance as Eddie.

I hate that smell.

So I didn't trust her.

* *

A few minutes later, it was time for me to get dressed for my Saturday-morning ballet class.

Claire: Go get ready in the bathroom! Quickly! Your grandmother will be here any minute!

I obeyed Claire's orders, and went into the blinding, all-yellow bathroom. I got dressed as fast as I could, then anxiously waited for my grandmother by the front door.

I need to get out of here.

Eventually my grandma pulled up in her old white Lincoln (like a knight in shining armor), and immediately, I tried running toward her. But Claire grabbed my right arm to hold me back, and whispered into my ear.

Claire: Don't you so anything to her, Layla. Do not let her find out you were a bad girl.

What did I do?

I knew for sure that I went to sleep alone, had a nightmare, then I woke up with Eddie holding me tightly.

What did I do wrong?

I didn't want anyone to think I was a bad girl.

Was I bad?

More than anything, I need you to think I'm good.

* *

When my grandma opepend the door for me, I had already decided I didn't want to get in trouble, or have her think I had done something wrong. So I got in, buckled my seat belt, gave her a kiss on the cheek, and decided to say nothing, as my mind continued to race with confusion.

Claire told me not to say anything, because grandma will be mad at me. And I don't want her to be mad at me.

For the most part, we were able to sit in silence, though she did ask me if I had a good time with Emily.

Me: Yeah I did.

No.

I did not.

Then at one point, she got a giant smile on her face.

Grandma: Well you'll be happy to know, I invited Emily to your birthday party tomorrow! Claire said, she and Eddie can bring her to the park after church...Ms. Soon-to-be-ten- years-old!

I can't wait for tomorrow to be over.

The rest of the car ride wasn't too long, just ten minutes total. But in those ten crystallizing minutes, I had forgotten almost everything from the most recent nightmarish morning; and without even trying, anything else I was unable to erase, I'd end up forgetting by the end of ballet.

I float away to places where no one can find me.

I love it here.

I like it when they tell me I'm good.

SURVIVING
IS FORGETTING

7

Maria: Then what happened?

Me: I don't know, I don't really remember. It's all kind of a blank after that...

Maria: Blank?... like, all the way blank?

Maria gets up to go get something to drink.

Me: Yeah all the way blank... up until Isabelle.

She yells out to me from the kitchen.

Maria: Isabelle who?!... Hey! Want some tea?! I'm making tea!

Me: Yeah I do! Isabelle Garcia! From middle school... my first kiss!

Maria: Oh! ...well this sounds like a super cute story! And lord I hope it is!... or is this as tragic as your other show-and-tell me about your sad-ass, blast-from-the-past stories? Be honest Layla!

Me: Oh it's tragic baby. Perfectly tragic, too.

ONIONS FOR ROSES

8

By eighth grade, I had not kissed anyone.

Why would you want to?

That was, until I met Isabelle Garcia.

Whoa.

Isabelle was the coolest girl in school, and cooler than any boy, by a long shot.

Isabelle Garcia.

It was the way she dressed like Aliyah, and how she wore this cherry-red backpack, with patches on it (Lauryn Hill, Lisa Frank, Bikini Kill). Then there were her faded, black converse shoes (with drawings scribbled all over them), and her daily, rotating neon-manicure.

She's so cool.

It was also the way she spoke very little.

I like that, too.

Isabelle Garcia.

She's perfect.

I wanted so badly to meet her.

She's too cool for me.

But then, on one astrologically aligned day, all the cosmic stars conspired in my favor, so that I could finally get my chance at an introduction to THE Isabelle.

Holy shit, it's her.

It was during winter break, at North Beach park, while I rode my royal blue bike, and she on her purple skateboard.

There she is!

I peddled as fast as I could to catch up to her.

Be cool.

Be cool Layla.

Layla! Be cool!

Me: Hi. Hey! I'm.. I'm Layla!... we go to school together.

Isabelle: Yeah. I know.

Me: I'm Layla.

Isabelle: Yeah you said that.

Me: Right!... right!

Isabelle: I'm Isabelle.

Me: I know!

Isabelle: Okay....

Me: I'm sorry, I just... I've noticed you before and I...

Isabelle: You noticed me?

Me: Yeah... once, or twice.

Isabelle: Once, or twice?

Me: Yeah.

Isabelle: Cool.

Me: Cool.

* *

Isabelle and I ended up spending that whole day on the beach together.

This is literally magical.

The entire time we shared her headphones, and listened to my Hole CD. Then, while I made her a friendship bracelet, she braided my hair... and as we walked each other home, we brushed hands for the first time.

I'm in love.

But after that, I wouldn't see Isabelle for another two weeks... not until the end of winter break.

I wonder what she's doing right now.

* *

Once the new school semester started, Isabelle and I flirted with each other every day (which meant we stared at each other intensely, and barely brushed up in the hallways between classes).

Whoa.

Then one day, Isabelle passed me a note on our way to first period.

Isabelle's note: meet in the west bathroom, 3rd period

I think we're going to kiss.

I hope I'm good at it.

As soon as I walked up to her, she took my hands, and pulled me into the fourth stall, then locked the door.

The first time I ever kissed a girl, felt like the first time I ever breathed air.

I fucking love third period.

We held hands the entire time we kissed.

Perfection is overrated.

Two periods later, Isabelle made out with Trevor Davis, by the eighth-grade lockers... in front of everyone.

In front of me.

Why though?

And that was that.

I had been dumped, without her ever having to say it.

But I love you.

＊ ＊

After that, I cried every day in school for a month. Actually, I cried so much that Trevor Davis, Isabelle's new boyfriend, got the whole school (including Isabelle), to start calling me: "onions."

I hate you.

Though when she said it, that was when I left my body.

Isabelle: Onions.

She doesn't exist.

That was when I floated out my body, and toward the comforting lyrics of Mariah Carey, once again.

Cause you'll always be my...

They don't exist.

By the next day in school, if anyone asked me, I didn't know who Isabelle Garcia was.

Who are you even talking about?

Isabelle Garcia.

She was truly the worst first kiss...

Never.

TEENAGE MUTANT FINGER SNATCHER

9

Maria bolts out of kitchen, with gusto.

Maria: Okay FUCK Isabelle Garcia!

I giggle, and Maria sets up our hibiscus tea with honey, while I finish rolling up a fresh joint.

Me: And you know what? The first boy I kissed was pretty fucked up too.

Maria: Hey, mine too, girl! Mine too. Fucking Brian whatever the fuck, I don't remember his last name. But that little shit, stuck his finger in me, without my permission, right after I kissed him. Like, chill! I didn't ask for all that. He fucked me up! Just like Isabelle fucking Garcia fucked you up. But like, in a different monumental way.

Me: And Cody.

I pass the joint to Maria.

Maria: ... who the fuck is Cody?

Me: Well my Cody sounds a lot like your Brian.

PLAY DEAD

10

One summer, my family and I took our annual trip to the Virgin Islands with The Porter's, and their oldest son, Cody Porter.

Hm... Cody.

Cody was thirteen, and so was I, but we hadn't seen each other since we were ten.

Whoa.

Cody.

Cody Porter...my new crush, and full on distraction.

Fuck Isabelle.

* *

By day two of our co-family vacation, Cody and I had declared our mutual crushes by sneaking off to the docks of the vacation house, and making out twenty-two times without getting caught once.

Making out is fun.

But by day five, we had agreed it was time to take things to the next level.

I'm getting bored.

So instead of making-out behind the docks (where no one was wandering), we decided to do it inside the enormous vacation house (where everyone was hibernating).

This is way more fun!

The rented home was a three story, island, mini-castle, painted soft blue, and built on stilts. It smelled like sunsets, saltwater, and Cody's mom's expensive floral perfume. There were six bedrooms, a private tropical garden, it's own mini-beach, two kitchens (outdoor and indoor), as well as a two-boat dock... plus two boats.

This place is insane!

Cody and I had too much fun making-out, in all the places our families could catch us.

Now this is exciting!

We even made a checklist.

I like this game.

Next on our make-out list: Living Room

* *

That night, we decided we'd tackle our newly designated secret-spot, after everyone went to sleep. However, before our lips could even touch, we wore ourselves out talking about the new Zelda level, and unexpectedly passed out on the couch. A couch, that was big enough to allow two thirteen year olds to spoon for the first time.

I've done this before.

* *

The next morning I woke up to a familiar feeling.

His hand is on my...

I opened my eyes, but the rest of me wouldn't budge.

I can't move.

My body felt a lot like it did in the pink room.

I can't move!

I finally remembered where I was, and who I was with.

Cody?

But before I could say anything, he whispered into my ear from behind me.

Cody: Layla? Are you asleep?

It's not safe to move…

I didn't respond.

… don't speak!

Instead, I let him believe I was long into dream land.

There are pieces of you inside of me, and I play like I like it. No one taught me to, or maybe someone did, and I can't remember who.

A few seconds later, Cody squeezed my breast.

Eddie?

Why I can't move?

There it was, Cody's sweaty hand, on my newly formed breast, touching my very cold nipple.

My heart is racing so fast!

I don't know what to do.

Cody's unexpected hand had become too much for my body to handle, so my mental auto-pilot turned on, and I floated right out of the room, toward another familiar song.

I'm just a girl, in the world…

…is he almost done?

But Cody's grand finally didn't come until he decided to shove his adolescent fingers right into me.

That hurts!

I felt his partially bitten nails, as they scrapped the insides of my sensitive skin, but I couldn't tell him to stop.

It's not safe.

It was the first time anyone had ever fingered me.

Who taught you to do this to me?

* *

The next morning, Cody didn't speak to me, he didn't even look my way during breakfast, but I already knew things weren't going to be the same after that night. I knew it from the moment he asked me: "Are you asleep?"

SMASH N GRAB

11

Maria sits in front of the mirror, and applies silver glitter to the tips of her perfectly lined blue eyeliner; while I lay on my back, staring at the ceiling-fan spin in circles.

Me: Did you ever say anything to the boy who stuck his fingers in you without asking, while he kissed you?

Maria throws down the makeup stick.

Maria: No! I mean... by the time I had the foresight to realize how disgusting he was, I had fully grown up, and couldn't even really remember his full name. Just fuck him. But! I do hope some grown ass woman smashes his face into the wall, if he's still out there pulling that shit.

Me: It's crazy how we just didn't... or don't stop them... or say anything. Right?

Maria: I don't know, I'd like to say I speak up now...I do for the most part, but being a teen... I mean it's a pretty weird time for everyone, isn't it?

Me: Well fuck! It most certainly was for me! Hey pass me that! My teen years are upon us. Woo!

Maria: Hold on! Let me light it back up for you mi amor.

I DOUBLE DARE YOU

12

For high-school, I ended up at a performing arts magnet program in downtown Miami, one that had fewer students than most.

Is this a good thing?

In total, there were four hundred and twenty-two artistically gifted overachievers, and I was proudly one of them.

This makes me feel special.

Everyone knew everyone, and everyone saw everyone.

This school feels like being in a fishbowl.

* *

I was half way through my freshman year, and feeling pretty comfortable at my new school.

I think I like it here.

In a short amount of time, I had made some new friends (not easy for me as an only child), I was mostly keeping up in my academic classes (which was a challenge for my dyslexia), and all my dance-classes were truly incredible (they were a dream come true).

This is just like the movie "Fame."

I can be happy here... I think.

And I was, for a while I was really happy.

I just want to be okay.

That was, until an ill-fated Friday that ran parallel to the book my English class was reading, "The Scarlet Letter."

On that Friday, while walking from Algebra to Spanish, my newest best friend, Robby Goldman, accepted a dare from their new friend, Derrick Allen.

Derrick's a dick.

The Dare: yank open my tearaway track pants

It all happened within seconds.

Please don't look at me.

Everyone's eyes were holding onto my humiliation.

Then I did it again. I left my body. It was automatic, just like with Eddie, Isabelle, and Cody. Though this time, instead of Mariah Carey, or Gwen Stefani, the angelic cascade of Kate Bush's voice amplified in my mind, and drowned out the heckle of laughter.

I should be crying, but I...

Public shaming feels a lot like self-shaming.

Everyone stopped.

Everyone looked.

Everyone laughed.

Including Derrick Allen.

And Robby.

Then the sound of the main stairwell-door, slamming shut, forced me right back into my body.

Please stop staring at me.

I urgently grabbed tight the open legs of my pants, and ran toward the back stairwell.

Stop!

Unexpectedly, Robby followed after me, who (after ripping open my pants) wanted to make sure that I was okay.

Really?

They didn't want to see me hurt, but they also weren't ready to admit to being the one who hurt me.

Robby: Are you okay?

Me: ...

Robby: Layla... don't be mad. Derrick dared me to!

So they had to.

So they did.

Robby: You're not mad right?

Me: ...

Robby: Come on... you know Derrick and I are always joking with everybody. It's not just you. Don't be like that.

Me: ...

Robby: And we did it cause we love you Layla!

Me: ...

Robby: Come on... Layla... please... it was just a joke.

I didn't know how to answer them.

Am I overreacting?

I sat in the stairwell, buttoning back up my pants, and trying to think of what to say to them. It was complicated; just like with my grandmother, I didn't want them to be mad at me. I didn't want to risk losing their friendship by telling them they had hurt me, and I really wanted them to still like me.

Robby's right.

I'm overreacting.

It was just a joke.

You're going to upset them.

Just tell them you're okay.

Robby: You're okay, right?

Be okay Layla.

Me: "Okay...yeah I'm okay."

I'm not at all okay.

WE'RE FESTERING

13

Maria: Honestly! I'm happy you finally talked to Robby.

Me: Well I did it because of you.

Maria: That was all you boo, but...well, I do remember you told me, but... you didn't tell me what he said afterwards...or wait! Was that, that night?

Me: Yeah...it was... and no I never did, did I?

Maria: No you didn't... but other things were happening, too. Way more pressing things to say the least.

Maria lights up the joint, takes a hit, and passes it to me.

Maria: Okay, well until you get to that charming part of the story...can we get back to high-school?! Because clearly that was super fun for you!

We laugh, and I take a hit.

Me: Oh yeah! High-school was a fucking blast.

I exhale.

LITTLE LADIES

14

Every morning, to get to school, I would walk eight blocks from the train station, to the front doors of my nine story high-school building.

I feel so grown up.

And on my way, I would stop at Mr. Loretto's Pizza Parlor; where I'd meet my friends, who had also walked the eight blocks from the same train station (different train).

We are totally, so grown up!

We would gather, daily, for a piece of his infamous pan con mantequilla, and a cortadito.

Yum.

Everyone loved the way Mr. Loretto would add extra butter on the pan, and the perfect amount of sugar in the cortadito.

So yum.

Plus, Mr. Loretto was really nice to us. He knew all of our names; he knew which one of us were a painter, an actor, or a dancer, and he would offer us free pizza at least once a week (usually on Friday's).

Dependability feels safe, even in the form of pizza.

Then one Tuesday morning, outside of our favorite pizza parlor, I saw my friends looking terribly confused.

Mr. Loretto's is closed?

There was no sign of Mr. Loretto.

Madison: I wonder where he is.

* *

Later that day, after getting home from school, I called Madison (who always knew everything) as soon as I could.

Madison: Layla! Mr. Loretto was on the news!

Me: What! Why?

Madison: His daughter is missing! The one who kissed David L, in front of Wet Seal... and goes to American High. She hasn't been home in two days! Like... two whole days!

Me: That must be why Mr. Loretto wasn't there.

Madison: I mean... probably. Yeah.

Then my mom yelled to me, from the kitchen.

My mom: LAYLA! LAY-LA! Get off the phone now! Time for dinner!

Me: I gotta go. I'll see you tomorrow.

Madison: Okay, I'll see you tomorrow... wait! Layla!

Me: Yeah?

Madison: Watch the news tonight.

* *

That night, I finished the rest of my homework in the living room, because I wanted to see Mr. Loretto on the television. I wanted to see it for myself. I wanted to see him. I wanted to see his daughter.

I've never seen someone I know on t.v.

Finally the ten o'clock news came on.

There she is.

Tatiana Loretto.

She looks my age.

All of the sudden, somehow, she was missing from my life too.

That night, the news Anchor told the story of how Tatiana never came home from school, and said that the police hadn't ruled it out as a runaway yet (even though they had shown footage of Mr. Loretto explaining how Tatiana picked up her younger sister, every day, from school).

Why don't they care about her?

According to her dad, the day Tatiana didn't come home, was also her Abuela's birthday (which she had helped prepare for). Therefore, it made no logical sense that she would actually run away, especially on that day.

I don't understand.

I watched Mr. Loretto continue to cry on the television, as he pleaded for information on his daughters disappearance.

Why won't they help him?

Then the news anchor startled me in my thoughts, when she concluded her series by saying:

"this young woman…"

Wait. What?…is Tatiana a young woman?

Am I?

I was obsessively trying to make sense of it.

Am I a girl, or a woman?! My mom is a woman, and so is my aunt…

My cousin is younger than my mom, and a little older than me, but she lives by herself, so she's a woman. And I'm fifteen, and Tatiana is fifteen…but we're not…girls?

Is that why they won't help Mr. Loretto find her? Is that why they won't help her?

I stayed up all that night, trying to make sense of my newly assumed title in the world, and worried for Tatiana.

I wonder if the news anchor is thinking about her too?

* *

The next morning, I woke up, threw on my denim overalls and red t-shirt, pulled half my hair up into a ponytail, put on my silver hoop earrings, grabbed my backpack, and ran out the door to catch my bus.

I'm late!

Then the bus dropped me off at the train station.

I wonder if they helped Mr.Loretto?

It was just like every other morning.

I wonder if Tatiana is okay.

But then while walking the traditional eight blocks, to the front doors of my nine story high-school building, I noticed Mr. Loretto's Pizza Parlor still looked closed.

I hope Tatiana is okay.

Unfortunately, I could also see that I'd soon be having to walk by three obnoxious men, standing outside of the fabric store, right next to Mr. Loretto's. At once, I saw that one of them was smoking a cigar, one of them was smoking a cigarette, and all three were holding coffee cups from the deli across the street.

Fuck!

I have to pass by them.

As I got closer, I could feel this knot tightening in my stomach, and my heart starting to race in my chest.

I hate the smell of cigarettes.

I clenched the straps of my backpack.

Man with a cigar: *whistles*

Man with a cigarette: Hello! Hello little lady! Mi mujer!

Man with a coffee cup: Damn girl! What a woman!

What should I say...is it safe to say nothing?

I said nothing.

Man with cigar: Hey! Show my friend some respect!

Fight or flight?

Fight or flight?

Fight or flight?

Without a thought, I took off running.

Don't stop Layla!

I ran for five and a half blocks, without stopping once.

Turn around to make sure they're not there!

Then I only slowed down to see if they had followed me.

Please don't still be there.

They hadn't. Instead, they had focused their attention onto the next girl.

Wait...

...woman.

It was Emily Lee, a junior, who majored in theater.

Woman?

She was sixteen (just a year older than Tatiana, and I).

What is the difference between a girl, and a woman?

On that day, Emily had been wearing a blue dress (with little orange flowers all over it), and her hair in two pig-tail braids (with hot-pink bow clips). And she wore makeup.

She's a woman?

* *

About a block west of Emily Lee, was Elena Suarez. Elena was fourteen years old, and wearing the same overalls as me... accept her's had a cartoon bear sewed onto the front pocket.

Okay I get it now...

Elena would soon have to pass the men in front of the fabric store, who were eagerly awaiting her approach. I could see her clenching her backpack straps, just like me, as the men began to whistle at her.

She...

... we...

... she's a woman.

WHEN TO ADULT ME

15

Maria: Hold on... what happened to Tatiana?

Me: My bad... it was actually pretty fucking terrible. They found her body a month later, off the Palmetto Highway. Some guy from her neighborhood did it, too. They also never referred to her as a kid. Just "young woman found dead". I'm telling you!... if you have a vagina, your least likely to experience innocence as a child.

Maria: Ouf!

For a moment we stay silent, while Maria takes a hit.

Maria: You know some people say girls become women when they get their periods.

Me: That's insane.

Maria: No I know, but I think everyone judges the age of girls based on our bodies evolution, which is fucked, because some girls get their period at like ... nine, and, or the biggest fucking titties! Like me! Who, in high-school wore sweatshirts everyday in Miami! Like thats so fucked up... that I had to wear a fucking sweatshirt in ninety-degree, humid ass, weather! Just to feel safe!

STANDING OVATION

16

In my high-school, there were a set of three elevators that all led to the main entrance (which was on the third floor...the main floor).

Breathe Layla.

The floor everyone entered, every morning.

This makes me so anxious.

* *

One morning, during my sophomore year, a group of fifteen boys collectively lined the main hallway of the third floor. And what they had so brilliantly decided to do (with this lining of virile energy), was to rate every girl with: APPLAUSE or BOOOOOOOO's.

Seriously... who taught them this shit?

They made it inevitable too, by standing right in front of the elevators, so that we had to walk by them. I mean, they had actually strategized the whole thing, as if it were a gender war.

I hate them.

I held my breath once I realized what was going to happen. My chest instantly tightened up, and the knots in my stomach made me feel sick. It was the same feeling I would get, when I had to pass the men in front of the fabric store.

I want to throw up.

I waited, and watched two other brave girls go first.

Shit.

One got a standing ovation; and the other got boo's, loud stomps, and balls of paper thrown at her.

I can't breathe.

The panic in me took over entirely. Before I knew it, I had fled back down the stairs, and into the first floor bathroom (which is where I spent all of homeroom).

I gotta get out of here.

After the first bell, I left school, and went straight to the mall.

I don't feel safe.

It was the first time I had ever skipped school.

I hate it here.

I hate being a girl.

JERKS NEED MIRRORS

Maria: Pendejos!

Me: So many pendejos.

Maria: It's because pendejos are insecure at that age. I mean, any age sometimes...but especially in high-school!

Me: I mean, I was pretty insecure in high-school too... actually, if I'm being honest, I still am.

Maria: Of course you are! Me too! Who isn't? Seriously. No one knows what's going on about anything anymore! But I'm saying...

Maria lights up the joint, and takes a hit.

Maria: I'm saying...when girls are insecure, they can be a danger to themselves...sure that's true, sometimes. But when those actual homophobic cis-boys are insecure, then mama, they usually aren't a danger to themselves...uh-uh! They for real become a danger to everyone else!

Me: Fuck...that's terrifying.

Maria: Indeed it is.

NON-CONSENSUAL
LOVE-BOMB

The second time I fell in love, I was sixteen.

Loving and escaping can be the same thing. Right?

* *

I first met him in high-school, during fall semester, on my way back from lunch. We bumped into each other while in the same stairwell (I was running up, and he was walking down). I remember I thought he was nice, because he stopped to help me pick up my books. I remember I liked the way he dressed (like Brad Pitt in "Fight Club"), and I remember I thought he smelled good. I didn't know what it was, but I knew I liked it a lot more than the AX the other boys were wearing.

He smells like he knows things.

I had never seen him before, yet based on what I heard from Chloe (a friend in the visual arts department), I thought I knew exactly who he was; especially once he smiled, and told me his name.

Him: Mr. Mills... but you can call me Drew.

It is him!

* *

Everyone in school had been talking about the new guest teacher, Mr.Mills. He was some big painter from New York, who was teaching the visual artists for the semester.

The rumor was, he was really hot.

He really is.

* *

The next time I saw Mr. Mills…

I mean Drew.

…was while on the train, heading home from school.

Oh my god.

I was immediately anxious, and nervous.

It's him again!

I watched him, as he softly looked over his left shoulder, and stood up for his stop.

Shit!

He saw me staring at him!

But then he smiled back at me.

Oh my god he smiled.

Smile back Layla!

So I forced a fake smile, and he waved at me with pity.

I can't believe he waved at me!

Preying on puppy love is pitiful.

* *

After that I didn't see Drew at school.

I wish I could see him right now.

He was a guest teacher for a different department than mine, so it put us in two separate wings of the building. Therefore, there wasn't a reason for us to be in the same place, at the same time... not really.

I wish there was.

Though I did think of him, every single day.

Drew.

And pretty obsessively.

I wonder what he's doing.

I wonder if I'll see him again.

I wonder how I can see him again.

Your job to distract me, from me, won't work if you're not here.

* *

That year, on the Saturday before Halloween, I went to the mall for some new lip gloss, and a CD. And as fate would have it, I would get to see Drew for a third time.

Oh my god, it's him!

There was Drew, standing in line at the pretzel stand.

He's so cute.

Then, just like on the train, he waved at me.

Oh my god.

He waved at me again!

I watched Drew get out of line, and walk over toward me, before even getting his pretzel.

He didn't get his pretzel!

Holy shit! He's coming over to me!

Oh my god!

Drew: Hey Layla.

Me: Hey...hi... hey... hey... Mr.Mills.

Drew: Drew. I told you, you can call me Drew.

Me: Cool, cool. Yeah, okay... yeah Drew.

Then Drew smiled at me.

He smiled at me again!

I had also noticed that he glanced down my body, before he spotted the bag I was holding from the CD store.

Holy fucking shit!

I think he just checked me out.

Drew: What CD did you get?

Me: Hole.

Drew went on to tell me about how he loved Hole, because his older sister had made him listen to them.

He's so cool.

He even asked what my favorite song was.

Me: Me? Oh uh, "Violet". I love that song.

Drew: Yeah, me too.

He totally gets me.

He was thirty-one.

Teens are too much for some to handle, and for others, teens are just right.

* *

The moment by the pretzel stand had me feeling so giddy, and I didn't think I could get any happier.

Oh shit... is he....

But then Drew wrote down his phone number, on a folded-up piece of yellow legal paper he had in is pocket.

Shit! He did!

And before walking away, he slipped it to me (just like my friend Heather had slipped me notes in Geometry).

Just like Heather.

Drew: Now don't tell anyone, especially your friends. They'd be so jealous of you, and probably never speak to you...especially Chloe.

He's probably right.

Chloe did say she thought he was cute.

Everyone did.

I called him that very night, as soon as I got home.

I can't believe he likes me... like... he likes me!

* *

In the following weeks, once my parents went to sleep, we talked nearly every night. He'd tell me about all the music he loved (Hole... just like me), his favorite movies (Aronofsoky's "Requiem For A Dream"...just like me), and the book he had just finished reading ("Choke" by Palahniuk)... also, just like me.

We have so much in common!

Then, for the rest of the semester, if I ever saw him in school (or on the train), I just pretended like I didn't know him. And just like he'd told me to, I never told anyone what was going on between us.

He really likes me... to go through all of this for me.

* *

Then the ultimate happened.

Oh my god.

It was during Christmas break.

I can't believe it.

On that day, I met Drew at the beach plaza, for a movie.

I wonder if we'll kiss!

He told me to meet him inside the theater.

I can't wait to see him.

So I did.

I can't believe he wants to see a movie with me!

For the entire movie, our knees touched.

God I hope he kisses me!

I was entirely consumed with anticipation.

Oh my god!

Then he finally did it.

He's kissing me!

And just a few seconds later he stopped to ask me:

"Wanna go to my car now?"

I think he wants to have sex with me.

Me: Okay.

So I followed him back to his rented compact, which was parked on the third floor of the garage.

I just want him to keep liking me.

Then while we walked, he stopped.

Drew: I'm going to walk ahead of you, like we're brother and sister, okay?

I'm an only child.

I don't know what that means.

So he walked three feet ahead of me.

Is that what that means?

He opened the car, and once we were in, I noticed the doors automatically locked us in.

I don't like that.

Drew turned the car on, drove up to the emptier part of the garage, and put his car into park. Then we moved to the back seat, he lifted up my skirt, moved my underwear to the side, and climbed ontop of me.

I feel like I'm not even here.

It was my first time having sex.

Why doesn't it feel new?

The whole time, he held my shoulders down against the cigarette scented fabric seats, while he pushed himself in and out of me.

I hate that smell.

Once I smelled the cigarettes, I simply left my body, and drowned out the cringing sounds of Drew's orgasm, with J-Lo, who had been serenading us on the radio.

My love…

…cost…

…did I just loose my virginity?

* *

That night, after getting home, I tried calling Drew.

Why isn't he answering?

It was the first time he didn't answer my phone call.

I need to talk to him.

I called eight more times that night.

Why won't he answer?

My calls went unanswered for the rest of Christmas break.

What did I do?

What didn't I do?

* *

By the next Semester, Drew's guest teaching for the visual arts department was over; and my friend, Chloe, said she'd heard he'd already gone back to New York.

What's wrong with me?

I never saw, or heard from him again.

Seriously!

What's wrong with me?

And no one, except for Drew and I, ever knew what happened... not even Chloe.

Thank god.

I prayed no one would ever find out, too.

There's something wrong with me.

I thought if anyone ever did find out, they'd discover one of my darkest, most embarrassing secrets.

I knew it.

I really am unwanted.

BEACHBALLS NEVER STAY UNDERWATER

19

Maria: So did anyone in school every find out?

Me: Nope.

Maria: Ugh! I hate Drew too. Fucking predator! Disgusting! He is just like my bother's boss. Also a disgusting motherfucker! Let's see...my brother was twenty-seven at the time, I was seventeen, and my brother's boss was...

Me: Thirty-seven?

Maria: Thirty-five, but wait... while we were together he turned thirty-six...so...

Me: And did your brother ever know?

Maria: Fuck no! He doesn't know about half the shit I did before thirty. Let alone when I was in high-school, or college! Girl! He'd faint on the spot.

I get up to get some more hibiscus tea and use the bathroom, while Maria grabs a nail file, and a bottle of green nail polish to do our nails.

PIRATE GIRL

20

For college, like many eager freshmen, I moved out of my house, and far away from anything I'd ever known, to live on campus in my [not so] brand new collegiate dorm.

I hope I like it.

My major: Bachelor in Fine Arts, Dance Performance

I can't wait!

Yet the humble four hour move, from 'Hola Miami' to 'Yeehaw Tampa,' was a bit of an unexpected culture shock.

Holy shit!

Cowgirls in bikinis!

That was until I made some friends (the cowgirls in bikinis), and let go of my incessant need to compare Tampa to Miami.

Okay Tampa.

⋆ ⋆

One of the things my girlfriends and I came to love about the city, was the annual Gasperilla Pirate Festival.

Oh shit!

Every January, we'd jubilantly join the city in honoring the pirate known as Jose Gasper, aka: Gasperilla. The amusing day included a real-life pirate invasion, followed by a parade, and a grand finale of pirate-themed parties.

I love Tampa.

For two years, we had been dedicated attendees, and even began creating our own pirate themed costumes.

That Year's Theme: Jack Sparrow meets Brittany Spears

* *

Later that October, Tampa's other annual night of costumed mayhem, Guavaween, was about to begin.

I love Guavaween.

And to save some money, we decided to recycle our Gasperilla costumes, and mixed up everyones looks.

I love these costumes!

However, by junior year, we were also living in the new co-ed dorms (which unknowingly would be lined with hallways that would remind me too much of high-school).

Here we go.

Everyday (not just on holidays), we were forced to pass by a predictably boisterous, and unnerving group of guys.

I hate them.

A group of reputable assholes, who (on the night of Guavaween) chanted out at us in perfect harmony.

Reputable assholes: *Titties! Sluts! Titties! Sluts!*

But we all ignored them, and kept on walking.

Fucking idiots.

Then Lisa, in an attempt to make us laugh, pulled out a flask (hiding in her titties), and came up with a fun drinking game for us to play.

The Game: Each time a guy taunts us, we take a shot.

I feel drunk.

* *

A short walk, and five shots later, we finally arrived at Guavaween.

Shit... there's a lot of people here.

It all happened so fast.

Where's Lisa?

One minute we were in a haze of fun...laughing, dancing, drinking, smoking, and singing; the next Janelle was screaming out for Lisa.

Janelle: LISA! HEY! LIIIISSSSAAAA!

Lisa was nowhere in site.

Janelle: LISAAA!

We all turned to walk against the stride of the parade.

All of us: LISAAAAAA!

Eve spotted her first, in front of the pizza parlor.

Eve: Lisa! Hey!

There she is.

We had finally found her.

Lisa was slouched against the wall, and looking down, with her arms wrapped across her ribs, and her ankles crossed over one another.

What happened to her?

Something was wrong, and we all knew it.

Is she okay?

Then Monica knelt by Lisa's side.

Monica: Hey... you okay? Are you sick?

Lisa didn't say anything, or even try to shift her glance from the ground up to Monica.

I know that look.

Monica: Lisa?

Eve put her hands on her shoulders.

Eve: Lisa? What happened?

I bet I know what happened.

Lisa changed her glance from the floor, up to Eve. Then she stood up, brushed her skirt, and softly asked us to walk her to the police station (which was just one block south).

Really?

Lori: Can you tell us what happened?

Lisa didn't say a word.

Alison: Lisa?

Lisa walked toward the police station, like a shell-shocked survivor on a mission, and we followed her as if we were a group of lost children.

Why are we going in there?

* *

We cautiously walked into the police station's main lobby, curiously assuming what Lisa would say, or do next. But no one expected her to go right up to the woman at the front desk, and say she had been raped.

What did she just say?

She just said it... so nonchalant, like she was ordering tacos, or a coffee.

Eve: What did she just say?

I can't believe she just... said it.

Then a large male officer, emerged from behind the desk, and walked up to Lisa and eyed her up and down.

Officer: Can I help you?

Lisa: Someone raped me behind the pizza parlor.

Shit...she said it again!

Officer: Okay...

Then he cleared his throat.

Officer: Which pizza parlor?

Lisa: Moreno's.

Officer: Okay, can you tell me exactly what happened?

He didn't even take her to the back, or anything.

Lisa: Um... uh, they... we... my friends and I, we were in the parade, and then um, then someone grabbed me...and, and um, they... they pulled me into the alley, behind Moreno's.

Officer: What do you mean "grabbed you" exactly?

Did he just make air quotes?

Lisa: Uh, someone grabbed my wrist... pulled me through the crowd...then I... then um, then they turned me around... threw me against the wall. It was fast... lifted my skirt, um... and put something inside of...inside of me.

None of us knew what to say, we just stared naively in silence... and in a confused state of fear.

Officer: Did you maybe recognize the person?

Lisa: No.

Officer: Did you see anyone in the parade tonight that you know? Maybe from school, or anything like that?

Lisa: I mean... everyone.

Officer: No one stood out to you, or said anything to you that might have been... memorable?

Lisa: No.

Officer: Well did you notice anyone looking at you?

Lisa: I mean... everyone was looking at everyone... Sir.

Officer: Well I'm just am pointing out, that you might have stood out in the crowd. It just looks like, you and your friends, could have garnered some unwanted attention tonight.

Lisa didn't say anything, but her brow did furrow.

Officer: Well... look at you.

Did he really just say that?

Lisa stared blankly at the policeman, while we blankly stared at Lisa.

What do I do?

I don't know what...

Then Lisa just walked out... she didn't even look back to see if we had followed her.

What a waste of time.

She looked so defeated, and incredibly numb.

I mean look at you?

No one said a word after that.

I mean look at us.

EVEN THOUGH THE WORLD IS TRASH

21

Me: You know, I think that was the first time I saw it happen to someone else.

Maria takes another hit, before starting the second coat on my toe nails, and then passes it to me.

Me: I mean, I didn't see it happen to her, but I saw her change from it… like I recognized it.

I take a hit, and put the joint down in the ashtray.

Me: Actually… I saw it in her right away, you know?

Maria: Yeah. I saw that look in you, too…I knew it right away. It made me want to talk to you. I knew you would get me… and I'd get you. But hey wait!… what about Lisa?!

Me: What about her?

Maria: How is she doing lately?

Me: We haven't spoken since college… but I mean, I bet she doesn't trust the police to help her anymore.

Maria: A reality. Damn. I hope she's doing okay now.

Me: Yeah. Me too.

We sit in silence for a moment, both thinking of Lisa.

Maria: Layla, you know what I was thinking? So like five years ago...no one talked about rape right? I mean, not like now. Think about it... there weren't any top ten series, with the metoo agenda sprinkled all over it.

I pick up the joint from the ashtray, and light it back up.

Me: So?... what's your point?

Maria: My point is, that before let's say 2018, if you told anyone that someone touched you, without you giving them your permission, it was presumed to be your fault. And! You'd be slut-shamed by the police, family, friends, the news, movies and like... everyone! So no one ever really wanted to say anything, or admit it ever even happened. It's just... I think... almost every girl I went to school with... I don't know, I just think something happened to all of us, but no one talked about any of it. We just grew up...and we grew up fucked up.

I take a hit, and pass it back to Maria.

Me: Honestly, I don't think much has changed.

Maria: So true! Damn that's really sad though... like where is the bat-man that fights off rape?... or bat-woman!

FISHNETS HAVE
SUPER POWERS

22

While in college, I learned I couldn't keep the hours needed to work at the local coffee-shop, and simultaneously fulfill my collegiate obligations...so I decided to try go-go dancing.

Why not?

A couple of the girls in the dance department at school had talked about it, and said it was a fun way to make money. Plus, when I looked into it, it worked well with my school schedule, and it did seem like it could be fun to get paid to play dress-up in sexy costumes, and dance all night long. Honestly, it just sounded like it'd be performing in any other show I'd already been in (as long as I didn't have to walk by any of the pizza parlors or boys from my co-ed dorm).

I'll ask Aisha, at least I'll feel safer.

* *

I got my very first gig, with help from my girlfriend at the time (Aisha), who was bartending at a new lesbian club opening up in downtown: The Lounge.

Holy shit!

I can't believe I'm doing this!

As I paced back and fourth in the tiny dressing-room, I anxiously counted the minutes I had left before my very first twenty-minute go-go set would begin.

How much longer do I have to wait?

I tried to keep myself distracted, by changing my costume for the tenth time.

Should I change again?

Of course I changed one more time.

This!

I had settled on a pair of black fishnets, a black sequin bra, a red bikini bottom, a pair of black high-top converse sneakers, two shiny silver garters under my butt cheeks, a gold belt from Hot Topic, and lots and lots of glitter.

Am I wearing too much glitter?

Then finally, I was called out to start my first set.

Shit! I need a minute.

I walked into the densely smoke-filled, intimately sized bar, and was overwhelmed by everything, and everyone.

This is a lot.

I wasn't a "club-person" per se, and I had the type of anxiety that made it difficult to find pleasure in large crowds... unless I was on a stage, and separated from it all.

Just get to the stage.

But while anxiously moving through the colorful crowd, I noticed her.

Whoa.

It was a tattooed super-Shiva hanging upside down, from the metal bars in the ceiling.

Holy shit.

She was wearing red fishnets, shiny rainbow suspenders, black shiny platform combat boots, a cropped white ribbed tank top, clearly pierced nipples, short black hair, a red page-boy hat, giant golden hoop-earrings, and flawless makeup.

She looks like a real life MAC model.

I was hypnotized, and in total awe, as I watched her crawl down from the bars, onto the vertical pillars, and back onto the stage.

Fuck she's amazing!

I walked up to the six foot statuesque wonder woman, and was at a true loss for words.

Take a breath Layla.

Charlie: Hi. I'm Charlie.

Me: Hey. I'm ... um Layla.

Charlie: You're the other girl dancing with me tonight?

Me: Yep.

Charlie: Then get up here, and dance with me!

Holy shit!

* *

About two hours later, the place was packed with queer people from all over central Florida; while Charlie and I danced non-stop, and made some pretty good money.

This is so fucking fun.

I love the escape of glitter, my people, and a stage.

I love this.

This feels safe.

Then at about 1:00 AM, and midway through The Pussycat Dolls "Buttons," someone screamed out:

"They're breaking into the cars!"

What's happening?

Suddenly the music stopped, and everyone froze. Within seconds, before I could wrap my head around what was going on, Charlie flew off the stage, ran out the side door, and stomped through the parking lot screaming out to the suspected thief.

Charlie: Hey! Hey! What the fuck are you doing?!

Wait!... should I?...

My instinct was to go after Charlie and help her, but as I chased after her, I could see Charlie (in her platform combat boots, and fishnets), running fearlessly after the person who had just broken into our cars.

She isn't scared of anything.

I could see she wasn't waiting for anyone to save her.

She's fuckin' fearless.

No one was sure whose car had been broken into yet, and neither did Charlie. But it didn't matter to her. All Charlie needed to know was they were wrong, and she would make sure they knew it.

She's a super-hero!

Charlie continued to run after the thief.

Whoa!

Charlie: Get back here you piece of shit!

She's amazing.

It's truly incredible to see a woman be completely fearless, while wearing fishnets, and platforms.

I had never actually seen anything like Charlie before. She was breathtaking, and unexpectedly inspiring. I felt reborn watching her.

I want to be like that.

Fearless.

She was truly unstoppable.

Go Charlie!

Until she wasn't.

Damn!

Charlie had tripped, and fell right into a giant pothole.

Oh no!

But nothing, or no one could stop her.

Shit!

She really is unstoppable!

Tenacious as ever, and completely focused on injustice, Charlie effortlessly crawled out the hole, and screamed at the car thief with all of her fighting spirit.

Charlie: You won't get away from me fucker!

I stared at her with stars in my eyes.

What is...

...is she...

...I want to...

...she's so...

She was exactly who I wanted, and exactly who I wanted to be.

I wish Lisa could've seen this.

ALL MY HEROES
ARE SLUTS

23

Maria: Oh Layla! I love when it's obvious that sexy equals power.

I laugh.

Me: Me too.

I get up, and go to the kitchen to grab a bag of peanut butter pretzels I had been eyeing for the past few minutes.

Maria: Off the top of my head… Betty Davis! I'm talking about Mile Davis's daughter, um…Peaches, Lil Kim, Mother Pamela Anderson, Anais Nin, Frida, Barbarella…

I come back with the bag of pretzels in my hand.

Me: Oh yeah, most definitely Jane Fonda now, then, and forever.

Maria: Fucking right. Rihanna, Monica Lewinsky, Maya Angelou, Anita Hill, Madonna, y la reina Selena…

Me and Maria: *Selenaaaaas.*

We laugh.

Maria: Honestly, every woman I look up to, and have the deepest level of respect for…I mean, they've all been slut shamed at some point. What the fuck?

Me: Right?!

Maria: Oh my God! You know who else is a queen? Ms. Candida Royale!

Me: Wait, who's that?

Maria: What?! Candida Royale! She is the first woman to start a porn company!

Maria reaches for the pretzels, and I reach for the joint.

Me: Oh fuck yeah.

I take a hit, shotgun Maria again, and she exhales.

Maria: Fuck yeah.

Me: Oh I almost forgot! Your new tattoo! Let me see!

Maria lifts up the bottom of her pant leg, to revel the outline of an elephant tusk, with the word "surrender" written below it.

Me: I love it.

TRAMP STAMP

24

When I was a teenager, a sweeping trend took hold of a number of females... the ever elusively infamous lower-back tattoo.

I want one.

And I would inevitably get mine because of the women I looked up to as if they were my older sisters, mentors, and gurus.

Janet Jackson - Drew Barrymore - Mariah Carey

I want to be just like them.

So by my fifteenth birthday, I had saved enough money to get my first one (and put my fake ID to use).

Finally.

I had proudly joined my band of sisters, and got my beautiful butterfly, lower-back tattoo.

I'm gunna be just like them.

* *

By my junior year in college, I was still loving my butterfly; and I'd earnestly acquired three more badges of pride.

Top of neck - Right forearm - Left wrist

Also by junior year, I finally learned that my first lower-back tattoo, had a very affectionate nick-name.

Seriously… where do they learn this shit?

It was brought to my attention when I bent over to pick up my basket of clothes in the laundry room, and two guys saw the thin layer of skin between the top of my skirt, and bottom of my shirt.

Guy 1: Nice tramp-stamp!

Guy 2: Bet you like it from the back.

My tattoo was indeed a tramp-stamp, and I was a tramp.

That's what this tattoo is?

I hate it.

Something that had once made me feel so powerful, was now making me feel so small.

* *

By senior year, I was giving less thought to any of my tattoos, and more focused on all things school (like taking a class with my favorite professor, Ralph Davis). He was a phenomenal choreographer, and the reason I chose to try college. He taught me modern technique, dance-history, composition, he was responsible for my scholarship, and he supported me when I came out as queer to my class.

He's so confident.

Since he was gay, and out, himself, it made it easy for me to go to him for comfort, and advice.

I hope I can be just like him one day.

So a part of me broke, on the day my grey sweatpants dropped a little lower than expected (during modern class), and Professor Davis sort of whispered to me something, that echoed the boys in the laundry room.

Professor Davis: Nice tramp-stamp.

Does he think I'm...

... a tramp?

At the end of class, I didn't say anything to him. I knew he only meant it as a joke, and I had delivered harsher jabs. Yet, I couldn't shake the feeling that he, Professor Davis, saw me as less then.

He does... doesn't he?.

It was hard to wrap my head around the juxtaposing emotions. I mean, I knew I had gotten that tattoo to feel powerful, but it now seemed like it made everyone else think of me as powerless, cheap, slutty, easy, a good time... and "here for sex only."

He actually thinks...

...that I'm less then?

Am I?

Is that how he see's me?

As a tramp?

I didn't know what to say, so I laughed. I even laughed so hard, that I got Professor Davis (and the entire class) to start laughing, too. It was just like in high-school, when Robby pulled my pants open, and everyone laughed.

Why did I do that?

Accept this time, I was the one who started it.

Please stop.

Please stop laughing at me.

WHAT DOES SAFE
FEEL LIKE?

25

Maria takes a hit, and exhales.

Maria: I feel like even if you don't have a tramp-stamp, you have a tramp-stamp... you know? I mean...can you imagine if I was able to take a walk by myself, anytime of day, even at night, and wear whatever the fuck I want, and not give a fuck, or worry about being harassed, shamed, or attacked. Like... can you imagine what it feels like to get dressed, leave your house, and not ever have to consider your safety , or punishment... based on what you're wearing? I mean really!... Shit. I bet you can't.

I grab the joint from Maria, and take a hit.

Me: I'd have so much extra energy! Also, my tramp-stamp would probably be called a... shit! It wouldn't even have a name! Fuck. You ever think that day will really come?

Maria: I don't know... I mean... maybe not soon, or even in our lifetime, or the next, or the one after that... it's like... so far progress is taking a long fucking time. But maybe one day, right? I mean... maybe... if we finally vote some legendary gems of this predatory island!

Me: A new reality hit series!... coming this fall!

UNWORTHY

26

I met David on a full-mooned Saturday night, in Downtown Miami. We were at an artsy abandoned loft, celebrating a mutual friend's twenty-something birthday. And at one point, while passing a joint, I noticed him holding a beer, and wearing faded jeans, with a killer smile.

Who's that guy?

After some beer, and mild eye flirting, I finally felt buzzed enough to walk over, and introduce myself. That was when I learned his name was David, and that he was full of quick-wit, and charm.

He's cute.

Then, somewhere between the beer, and weed, he kissed me.

No one I just met, ever kissed me before… like that.

So I invited him back to my apartment for sex.

Let me try this sex-positive thing.

This IS sex-positive right?

I wanted to see if it would make me feel powerful, like all those heroes I'd seen on screen, or Charlie, but it didn't.

This is nothing like that.

It wasn't bad. I was just really nervous, and felt like I was inclined to perform for him, so I couldn't even cum, but... I definitely made sure he thought I did.

I want him to like it...

...I want him to like me.

* *

Five weeks later, David and I were still fucking, and texting. He loved to tell me about all the interesting facts he knew, and things he could do. He also loved asking me, about me. He wanted to know about my past, what I liked, what I didn't like, and somehow, he could relate to almost everything I was interested in.

He kind of reminds me of Mr.Mills...

...I mean Drew.

Ignoring intuition can prove to be unwise.

* *

A year later we were a couple, and living together (in my apartment).

He never wants to be without me.

It wasn't something we ever talked about, he just slept over one night, and then he never left.

I don't want him to leave me.

But to be honest, being with David had become a sort of living hell, and I was becoming exhausted.

I'm so drained.

Dating him was a rollercoaster.

He's not always like that.

I was happy... sometimes.

Why is he like that?

But his inconsistency was wearing on my confidence.

Does he even like me?

David would say things to me like:

"That's what you're going to wear? Come on."

"Look at you. You wonder why I look at her?"

"No one likes an angry woman."

"You're getting old, and no one will want you."

I was twenty-five.

"You're crazy to believe her...she's just jealous of you."

"Come on honey, you should try to be more sexy."

"You don't ever care about me, or what I need."

"Your butt could look better, if you tried harder."

"You're going to need a boob job, your tits sag some."

I'd love to say I fought back whenever he said those awful things to me, but I wasn't that particular "she-ro" yet.

I need him to like me.

His truth was overpowering mine.

At the time, I couldn't imagine identifying that his words were abusive. To me, his words were just David being David, and I thought that my submission was me telling him I loved him. And I believed making sure that he knew I loved him, was all that mattered.

Does he not know I love him yet?

I need him to know.

My loyalty to loving him, cost me my self-love.

I was so confused, and I had lost all trust in myself.

I hate myself.

What was even more confusing than him assaulting my worth with his words, was how he would say it with care, with his hand gently on my shoulder, or my lower-back. Sometimes he would even do it with an empathetic look in his eye, or charming tone in his voice.

It's my fault.

I was certain he was doing me a favor.

I deserve this.

I'm not good enough yet.

* *

In a further attempt to win over his approval, I submitted my body to him.

Maybe this will work....

Whatever he wanted, I would give it to him.

I couldn't tell if I loved him, or hated him.

He never asked me what I liked... he would just remind me that if I loved him, I would do it. So I did it. And I did everything he wanted to do.

It doesn't hurt.

I even did the things that would hurt me.

It doesn't hurt!

Anal - Hogtied - Wood Paddled

It really hurts.

And none of it was kinky like in porn, or movies... it was violent. It was scary. It was like, the more pain he knew I was in, the more he liked it, and the more it turned him on... and the harder he would cum.

This is what I deserve?

Fuck!

This hurts!

I'd cope with the physical pain, and forget it was even happening by singing one of my internalized pop songs.

My loneliness, is…

Just like with Eddie, Isabelle, Cody, and Drew… my mind became a jukebox, filled with songs to defend my senses.

Give me a sign…

Are you hurting me, or loving me?

The irony was most present during our moments of romance. The ones that were the antithesis of the worst with him. The ones that kept my mind spinning, trying to understand his madness.

I'll take the five minutes of you at your best, even though I know I'll have to endure five days of you at your worst.

We would explore museums, laugh at movies, dance in bars, kiss at parties, skinny-dip at the beach, and chase sunsets on our bikes.

Please love me.

Isn't this love?

But the good never lasted long.

I know he loves me.

* *

We were finishing up dessert, at our one-anniversary dinner, and David smiled at me.

David: You're sexy, but you'd be even sexier with another woman.

I'll never be enough.

Followed by…

David: If you love me, you'll do it.

Kicking me when I'm down, leaves an extra loving bruise on my heart.

So that following Friday, I decided I'd try to prove my devoted love, by agreeing to a threesome with him (which would be my first time having one).

Fuck it.

I like women anyway.

But does he want this because I'm not enough?

Am I enough?

* *

Once we arrived at the dimly lit bar, we ordered some drinks, danced a bit, ordered another round of drinks, danced some more… and then, I saw her.

She's beautiful.

She wore a tight red dress, with long black hair, and black cat-eye glasses. I even pointed her out to David as soon as I saw her, but then she started to walk toward the exit.

Shit.

We watched as she moved through the jam-packed bar, and realized there was no way we were going to make it over to her before she left.

Me: Shit. She's leaving.

David: Her?

Me: Yes her. She's gorgeous, and she's leaving!

David: I know her! I'll just text her.

Me: You know her?

David: Yeah, from school.

Me: Really? Then text her, and tell her to come back in!

I was feeling confident...and I'd had a few drinks.

David: Okay.

Me: Did you text her?

David: I just did.

Me: Did she write back?

David: Not yet.

Me: Now?

David: Why don't we have a drink while we wait...try and calm you down a little bit.

Me: I'm fine... but a red wine please.

David: Let's get you something stronger...tequila!

Me: Okay, fine.

David couldn't get the bartender's attention, and I could tell it was starting to bother him.

Me: Do you want me to order?

David: No. I got it.

Me: Okay.

The bartender continued to ignore David.

Me: Did she text back yet?

David: Who?

Me: The girl... the one you know from school.

David: Not yet.

Me: Are you sure?

He was laser focused on getting the bartender's attention, and proving to himself that he was important. So much so, that he could think of nothing else.

David: Here... text her yourself.

He handed me his phone.

What the fuck?

It turned out he did text her... a few times.

David's text: hey sexy

Her text: hi ;)

David's text: send pic, I'm horny bb

I scrolled up and sped-read, four months worth of texts between David, and the mysterious lady in red... whose name turned out to be, Tabitha.

Wait... was I set up?

I read that they'd met to have sex several times a week. And, just like with me, David liked all the things that she liked, which were none of the things I liked.

What the fuck does he like?

I thought the bar had fallen silent, but it was just me, and at least a whole minute passed, before he even realized that he had handed me his phone.

Did he hand me this on purpose?

As soon as he did, he snapped it right back, and stared at me with the widest eyes I had ever seen.

Me: You know her?

David: Who?

Being lied to, by a liar, sounds just like the truth.

That was the first time I caught David cheating on me. But I gave into my need of being loved by him, and chose to believe his apology... which sounded a lot like a lie, which he made sound a lot like the truth. So I stayed with him, even though something deeper in me wanted so badly to leave.

I hate him.

I hate me.

* *

The second time I caught David cheating was about a year later, and I almost got stabbed right before it, too.

David!

On that weekend David and I, along with a friend and her boyfriend, drove down to Key-West for a mini getaway.

I hope he has a good time.

That weekend we smoked blunts, danced in the streets, drank at a nude bar (where the customers got naked) got dances at a nude bar (where the strippers got naked) bought purple wigs, got kicked out of two bars (no one remembered why), ate delicious Cuban food, and had lots (and lots) of drunk sex.

I'm glad he's happy.

Then, on our last night there, after my friend and her boyfriend went off to bed, David got extremely mad at me for the way I made his drink, and thought it best to put me in my place by:

 FIRST: holding me in a choke-hold

SECOND: throwing me into the wall

THIRD: putting his pocket-knife to my belly

Me: David stop!

My friend and her boyfriend ran downstairs to see what was happening.

David: She drank too much, and now she's attacking me! She won't stop! She's crazy! She tried to hurt me! So I had to defend myself! Guys she lost it! Look at her!

Look at me?!

I couldn't move or speak.

It's not safe.

Luckily, my friend's boyfriend got David to put the knife down. Then David, my friend's boyfriend, and my supposed friend, collectively blamed his erratic behavior on him doing too much cocaine, and mine on drinking.

I barely drank tonight.

[Not] my friend: He just did a little coke. Just let it go.

Why is SHE defending HIM?

This is when I found out that not all women side with women, and that David was even into cocaine (which was about six hours before I found out about Lynette).

Who the fuck is Lynette?

The whole drive back, was a six hour blur.

What just happened?

* *

As soon as we arrived back in Miami, we were greeted by Lynette, who was standing like a club-bouncer, outside my front door.

Who's that?

Lynette: Is this why you never came home? You lying motherfucker!

Apparently Lynette was under the impression that David was her boyfriend, and he was cheating on her... with me.

His girlfriend?

Who the fuck am I?

How did she even figure out where I live?

Wait...how did...

...wait, doesn't he live with me?

Lynette thought that she caught him red-handed, coming back from a getaway, with his mistress... me. Then Lynette ran away crying, and David chased after Lynette.

Why don't you love me?

* *

I stayed with David for another eight months after that, and Lynette did not.

Why do I let you do this to me?

I think it was because Lynette loved herself, and I hated me.

Without your love, I am nothing.

A NOIR SHADE OF LIGHT

27

Me: Sometimes the dark feels warmer than the light.

Maria: What?

Me: What?

Maria: What did you just say?

Maria laughs at me.

Me: I just think sometimes, it feels better to sit in complete darkness, it's like a warm blanket.... it feels warmer than the sun.

Maria: Layla! What the hell are you talking about?

Me: I don't know, I'm disassociating from David.

Maria: Okay therapy!

Me: Hah! Hey, pass me my phone. Please. I'll order us some food. I want to keep talking, but I also want food. What are you in the mood for? Thai again?

Maria: Mmm.

CHEAP SHOT

28

Once I finally left David for good, I spent the next year or so looking for people who would help boost my confidence, which still felt like it had been broken into a million pieces.

The necessary antidote:

1) Fuck someone new.

2) Fuck someone nicer.

3) Fuck anyone that isn't David.

4) Fuck anyone that doesn't look like David.

5) Fuck anyone that doesn't smell, walk, or talk anything at all like David.

Why is the antidote to fuck someone?

* *

After a few months of solid depression, I finally got it together enough, to mindlessly go out with some friends in search of a distraction... which is where I met Andrew.

He's cute enough.

He didn't look a thing like David.

He'll be perfect.

* *

An hour later, I was still dancing with David.

I mean Andrew!

Shit.

It was Andrew's dancing, and my mild desperation to replace the feeling of David's horrific memory, that led me to think:

I want to have sex with him… tonight.

Now.

I didn't want to stop feeling good, and it had been a while since a man wasn't making me cry, or feel like shit.

Andrew: Wanna get out of here?

Let's go.

* *

When I pulled up to his waterfront ultra-trendy condo, I realized I hadn't had sex, or dated anyone like that in quite some time.

Yeah… this will do.

With David, it was myself (and Lynette) that had become his financial supporter(s) over the course of our relationship(s)…so seeing someone have their shit together (financially)… was really turning me on.

I hope he makes me forget.

* *

The next morning, I woke up in Andrew's bed, to see the most beautiful sun shining through his floor-to-ceiling, hurricane-proof windows.

What is that?

I also woke up to Andrew.

Is that…

He was behind me.

…him?

And fucking me.

Cody?

I instantly felt like I was thirteen again.

Eddie?

I felt like I was eight years old.

I feel so small.

All I could do was remain lifeless, and turn up the volume on my mind's silent stereo.

Cause you'll always be my…

Don't move Layla! It's not safe.

This feeling of you inside of me, feels like nothing at all.

I asked myself if it was possible, that he had asked if I was asleep (like Cody did). But since I was actually asleep this time, I couldn't really say for sure.

Shit.

Yet, I did know for sure that he finished.

He's exactly like David.

I felt it drip down my back.

LOOK WHO'S WATCHING

29

Maria: I'm telling you. It's just like the guy I caught fucking me in my sleep on Angelica's baby monitor, while she was asleep right beside me! And you know, the sad thing is, I feel like other guys have done the same thing!...I just didn't have a baby monitor yet.

Me: Fuck. That is truly depressing.

Maria: I know.

There's a knock on the door.

Maria: I mean... the guy I'm with now... he would never pull that shit with me. I know it for a fact.

Me: And how are you so certain Maria?

She gets up to open the door, and the pad-thai that had just been delivered.

Maria: Because I showed him the knife I keep under my bed, and Angelica's baby monitor.

Me: Jeez! You're like some Mossad undercover goddess in the night... with a new-born in your left arm. Fuck Maria! You remind me so much of Selma!

KINKS FOR CASH

30

She shines bright like gold, and her rays beaming onto me, feels like basking in a luminous rainfall.

...that's Selma.

Other words that came to mind:

Whimsical

Iridescent

Incendiary

Genius

Kind

Beautiful

Hilarious

Unpredictable

* *

One afternoon, I stopped by my best friend's, for some of her baba ganoush, pink bubbly, and a little chat about her once-upon-a-time career as a stripper.

I wonder what it was like for her.

Selma had once surprised me by talking casually about her time at The Booby Trap, a popular Miami strip club.

Really?

Selma?

But I mean...she was a biochemist engineer.

And a government contracted arms dealer.

The CEO of a vintage couture auctioneer company!

And...

...stripper.

Okay yeah... Selma was a stripper.

Honestly, the idea of her being a stripper wasn't too shocking, once I let it sink in.

She's like Nomi Malone in "Showgirls."

Selma was this sort of illusive unicorn like human, who had the ability to create the world she wanted to be in, in every waking second of her life. She was fearless, brilliant, and lived her life with eyes wide open, searching for a way to satisfy her every curiosity.

Of course she was a stripper!

She was bold.

Whoa.

For example, when Selma was just nineteen, she convinced this guy (who was twenty-something) to buy her a roundtrip ticket (to and from Japan), where she snuck off, made new friends, left the twenty-something year old behind, and tried blowfish for the first time.

Whoa!

She once showed me the pictures.

It's a real blowfish!

Another time she flew off to Malaysia for a few weeks, paid for in full, by a charming Irish Poet who she met on Instagram, and charmed for a few months over DM's.

But what if…

When I'd asked her if she was worried about the poet being weird, or a murderer, Selma just giggled.

Selma: I'm the one running this… not him.

I wanna be like Selma.

* *

I walked into Selma's house, and took a deep breath in.

Mmm…

The instant smell of antique-wood, black coffee, vanilla candles, and wild poppy perfume tickled my nostrils.

I love her smell.

I entered her living room, and looked around at all of her surrealist paintings (painted for her by her friends), her one of a kind furniture (often collected from others front yards), and even more one of a kind knick-knacks (picked up on her unique global trips).

What's that?!

There was always so much to see in her house, so much so, that being in there felt like the first time, every time.

I've never seen that before..

I made my way to the kitchen, and Selma had chilled a bottle of pink champagne, prepared her fresh baba ganoush, aand a joint rolled just for me.

She's the best.

There was also music coming out of her gold glittered speaker, playing her carefully curated playlist.

Mozart's - "The Marriage of Figaro"

Lil Kim's - "The Notorious K.I.M"

Bjork's - "Human Behavior"

I love how it sounds in here.

I took a hit of the joint, a bite of the delicious baba ganoush, and walked toward her bedroom.

Me: Selma! You here?

Selma usually left the front door unlocked.

I wished she locked her door.

It was a habit of hers that always amused me, yet terrified me at the same time.

Me: Selma!

Selma: Layla! Hi! I'm here! I'm in my bedroom! I'm trying on the dresses I got from Etsy!

I walked into her bedroom.

Me: I love that dress! It looks amazing.

Selma: Awww, thankies. You can borrow it anytime.

I giggled, and lovingly mocked her.

Me: Thankies.

Selma giggled.

Selma: Did you get some yummy bubbly? I left everything out in the kitchen for you. There's a joint for you, too.

Me: I did. Do you want some? It's open.

Selma: Yes please.

I grabbed the bottle from the kitchen, then walked back into her bedroom to see that Selma had already changed into another dress. A vintage looking, vibrant blue a-line dress with black lace lining down the back.

Selma: Do you like this one?

Me: I do.

Selma: Me too. This one was cheaper though. Hah!

While Selma tried on a fourth, fifth, and sixth dress, we spent some time talking about her new favorite Etsy store, and her new crush (Maggie), while we finished half of the champagne, and baba ganoush.

Selma: I need a cigy.

I followed her outside.

I hate the smell of cigarettes…but I love Selma more.

We walked out to her backyard (which gave the inside of her house a run for its money), and I breathed anticipation into my chest.

This place…

…so Selma.

For example, there was a very scary baby-doll riding a bright orange dinosaur toy, a1950's gynecological chair, and a guillotine (which she used to chop open coconuts)…all of which she got from Bargain Barn, in Wynwood.

I hate that doll.

Selma giggled as we walked past the baby-doll, because she knew how much it scared me.

Selma: Don't worry Layla, she doesn't bite.

Me: Fucking doll.

In the midst of all that beautiful terror was a plush, red chair (which Selma sat in to smoke her cigarettes), and a royal-blue chaise-lounge (which I would sit in to smoke my Selma-rolled joint).

I do have fun here.

I gotta ask...

I took a hit.

Me: Selma...when you were stripping, how did you let everyone touch you? Like that... like how?

Selma smiled, and took a drag of her cigarette.

Selma: First of all, I didn't let everyone touch me. I allowed people who paid me to touch me. And believe me... I always was the one to choose whose money I wanted.

Me: What's the difference?

She took another drag of her cigarette.

Selma: There's a difference.

Me: I wouldn't know how to do that. I'm too... feminist.

Selma: Self-righteous much, my friend? I'm a feminist okay! Don't believe those lies about strippers! And, it can actually be fun seeing how much money men are willing to pay just to touch your boobs. I mean, this is money some of them lose sleep over earning, and money they might spend their lives making! And then they want to spend it on the illusion of sexual control, and sometimes a kink....

She takes a drag of her cigarette, and moves her sunglasses back up over her nose.

Selma: ... so if I'm ethically, and safely exploiting that, for my own financial gain, and independence...well, that's a feminist fuck you to the patriarchy dear.

At this point, I found it difficult not to trust Selma's logic.

She can brilliantly define the definition of reason, with her reason, every time.

Me: I just think if a stranger were touching my boobs, I would slap their hands away.

Selma: No. No way. I don't think so.

Me: But really... I would.

Selma: But you might not, not as a stripper. Because it's your JOB, like acting. And, they would've paid you whatever you think your boobs are worth... and you know, you might not be mad with money, and new found power.

Me: I...

Selma: So yeah, maybe you realize they shorted you, or maybe you think you should've asked for more... then yeah... then you might slap their hand away. But not if you said: "it'll cost you $100," then they pay you $100, just to touch your boobs for one song. Or... however long you decide to let them. That's a $100 toward your downpayment on YOUR house, or YOUR car! It's financial freedom.

Me: The fuck?

Selma: What?

Me: A man isn't going to pay me $100 to touch my boobs for two fucking minutes.

Selma: Yes he will.

Me: No way.

Selma: I mean, not every man, but some... yeah. And some women. People with expendable cash love paying for things... it helps them feel more powerful, or they just need to fulfill a need their scared to ask for. Even people without any extra money! Sex comes with a lot of shame Layla! And sometimes paying a stranger is worth that bag, instead of risking being made fun of, by your lover. Honestly... as a stripper, you're just feeding a real need. Supply, and demand baby! It's basic economics.

Me: Bullshit.

Selma: No bullshit. Better than that...you might see how much power you actually have, too.

Me: Selma! You're saying the only way to have power, is to let a man pay me to touch my boobs?... come on! That's the antithesis of feminism!

Selma: No it's not! My body, my choice.

That was close to a Selma check-mate.

Me: So you're saying that in order for me to feel powerful, I have to let strangers pay me, to touch me."

Selma: That's not what I'm saying. But as a woman, it is still statistically harder for you to get a job that pays as well as it would a man, and so, some women need to exploit the loopholes that allow them to make as much money as men, and remind themselves they don't need men to survive, or reach their financial dreams! Or they just simply do not have any other option available to them, and survival is real. So whether it's extra cash from being an Influencer, a fitness instructor on Onlyfans, or a stripper - all of these things are helping empower women financially. Plus, a whole lot of sex-workers go on to become CEO's, successful entrepreneurs, big time producers, and like BOSS-ES!

That was a Selma check-mate.

What can I say?

Selma: You don't believe me?

Me: I mean, the last part yeah... I get you. But I don't believe anyone will spend money just to touch my boobs.

Selma: Okay... watch.

Selma picked up her phone, and called someone named: Dylan.

Selma: Hey Dylan. Wanna come over and do coke off my boobs? And my friend Layla's?... $300 each.

$300 each?

Coke on my boobs! ... who's Dylan?

Selma: Be here in thirty minutes?... Cool.

Then she hung up.

She's serious?

Me: Selma... are you for real?

Selma: Yeah. Dylan loves titties, and cocaine. And he's very, very rich. Do you want some more bubbly, while we wait?

Me: Yes.

Shit I'm scared.

* *

In the forty minutes it took for Dylan to drive to Selma's house, I smoked a whole other joint, and passionately guzzled two and a half more glasses of pink-bubbly.

I can't be sober right now.

While we waited for him, I tried to keep my anxiety at bay, and stop thinking about this Dylan dude.

$300, in three seconds...that's my...

Internet bill.

Light bill.

Rent.

What if I just don't...

Me: Hey... what if I don't like it as much as you do?

Selma: Listen, if you get uncomfortable, at all, or anything like that... just say so. Squeeze my wrist, or give me a wink, and we'll stop. Right away. I promise. Okay?

Me: Okay.

Though some know her for her recklessness, for me, it's her willingness to be reckless, that makes me trust her most.

＊ ＊

I was startled by the sound of Dylan's large, beige, and expensive car, pulling into Selma's driveway. I was nervous, drunk, and stoned...just enough to pretend that I could breathe, and just enough not to care.

Fuckin breathe Layla.

The front door opened, and as Dylan walked in, I took one more large sip from my glass.

Dylan: Hi. I'm Dylan.

Me: Hey. I'm Layla.

As Tears for Fears "Head Over Heels" played on the gold-glitter speakers, Selma told me that she and Dylan had know each other for ten years, and that they'd done this twice before.

I'm safe.

I focused on the song lyrics.

... and talk about the weather.

Dylan stood casually in the doorway of the living room.

Dylan: So you said $300 each, right?

Selma: Yep. Three for me, and three for Layla.

Dylan: Here you go.

Then Dylan handed Selma six one hundred dollar bills.

Just like that.

There it was, just like Selma had explained it to me, a rich man with expendable cash, about to enjoy paying two women to see their boobs... and the ability to snort a line of cocaine off of them.

Dylan: Selma, can I get a drink first?

Selma: Sure. I have some bubbly, and scotch…

Dylan: Scotch.

Selma: Help yourself. It's on top of the fridge.

Dylan went to retrieve his manly drink, and Selma suggested we have our tits out for him, for when he got back.

Okay?

She had spoken about how the element of surprise was: "sexy, and salubrious". So the two of us sat down side-by-side on her couch, leaned back, and pulled down the front of our tops, exposing our breasts.

Certainly sexy, and salubrious enough for Dylan.

As he walked back into the living room, he looked over at us, and moved toward us like a tittie-zombie. All he could focus on were nipples, and the spot on our cleavage he would soon do his lines off of.

Selma: Come on Dylan. Don't you want to put it on us?

Obviously.

Then Dylan pulled out a small plastic bag of cocaine from his front beige pant pocket, and walked over to us.

Wow. He's ready, ready.

Selma: You can do one line off of each of us.

Dylan: How about two?

Selma: Two! You want to do four lines of coke… at 3:30 in the afternoon… on a Wednesday?

Dylan: Indeed I do, Selma.

Okay?

Selma: Then you have to pay each of us another $100.

Dylan: I'll pay whatever you want.

He likes being told what to do.

Selma looked at me, to make sure I was okay.

I'm okay.

Selma: Fine, but money first.

Dylan handed each of us another $100 in cash.

Selma: Well come on! We're ready!

I'm ready.

* *

As quick as it once took to get my ear pierced at Claire's, Dylan had done two lines of cocaine off of our boobs.

That's it?

It was over, it had tickled, lasted fewer than ten-seconds, and was easier than working an entire week as a barista.

That was nothing!

Finally, once he finished, Dylan wiped his nose, stood up from his knees, and said to us:

"Well thank you ladies...Selma, always a pleasure."

Seriously?... $400, for sitting here... and having boobs.

It was so easy, that I actually broke out in laughter.

Thats's it?

... for real?

And then before he walked out the door entirely, Dylan stopped to look back at Selma and I (who could not stop laughing), smiled at us with the biggest ear-to-ear grin, and yelled out as he shut the door:

"Co-caaaaaaaaine Tittiiiiiiiies!"

PAINTING OVER REGRET

31

Maria and I finish most of the pad-thai, and sit side by side on the couch, allowing the weight of our full belly's to anchor us down.

Me: That was about two months before she...

Maria: Wait...was that the last time you saw her?

Me: No...I wish it was.

Maria: ... the worst feeling.

Me: Wish I could trade it in... switch it out. You know?

Maria leans her head on my shoulder.

Maria: Yeah I feel like that about my brother. I just wish he... we... I mean... me... I just wish...

Me: It was different?

Maria: Exactly. I wish it was different.

Me: Yeah. Me too.

WWSD

32

I found out I was living in fear, and surviving it through avoidance, on one fateful New Year's Day.

It came at me like a fucking anvil.

Help.

On that most unforgettable day, I was forced to face one of my biggest fears... loosing Selma.

I can't believe it was suicide.

I can't believe she used a gun.

Time can make you want to run away as fast as possible... or simply freeze it forever.

The moment I found out (via text from her roommate that found her), I could feel my body crumble. It felt as if my bones were ripping open my stomach and heart, at the same exact time. It was excruciating.

Selma!

I screamed like I had never screamed before.

Seeeeeelmaaaaa!!!

I was simultaneously filled with regret, and guilt that pulled me down, like a two ton anchor dropping into the deepest, and darkest ocean.

Please help me.

I had lost someone I loved before. I even held my grand-mothers hand as she took her last breath, but nothing like this. This wasn't the kind of death anyone really likes to talk about, or pre-pares you for.

Make it make sense.

The brutal realization of our fragility, is fragile.

So when the unexpected consequence of shame, and guilt, fell onto me... that's when it all became paralyzing.

Selma.

I didn't blame myself, it wasn't that simple. However, I could not stop replaying in my mind, the last time I ever spoke to her... which would be the last time I ever saw her.

Is this loop a nightmare?

* *

The last time I saw Selma, was the first time I ever closed the door in her face.

Make it stop.

On that day (when she showed up unannounced), we had been arguing about her ignoring her depression (which I didn't fully understand), and I was scared to tell her she was beginning to drain me dry. Subsequently, I was also avoiding the reality that Selma didn't want my help, and there was nothing I could do about it. So I told her she should've texted, and then I closed the door in her face.

I don't know what else to do, anymore.

I have a masters, doctorate, and PHD in avoidance.

However, since I couldn't admit any of this to myself, I told myself a very believable lie.

I'll text her in a couple of weeks.

I told myself that through this supposed text, I would be able to avoid an uncomfortable conversation in person, not risk losing her friendship, and feed my hope of Selma one day overcoming her demons.

Selma, please...

But I never sent that text, and I never saw Selma again.

We lost her.

Her ways were ways that I've never seen before. And I don't think that I'll ever see them again.

* *

During the highest tides of my grief, I tried to avoid the pain of missing Selma by living out pieces of her life.

Where is she?

Some ways were more subtle, like wearing her giant Jackie-O sunglasses, eating Baba Ganoush, and drinking pink bubbly.

I need you.

Other ways were less subtle, like learning how to shoot a gun, and becoming a stripper.

Please come back.

Surprisingly, shooting the gun wasn't scary. I think I actually needed to do it. It was like, some dark, twisted, and beautiful thing that made me feel closer to her.

Is this what it felt like?

Yet the strip club... that was entirely frightening for me.

What will everyone think of me?

How did Selma do it?

I had toyed with the idea of stripping before Selma died... especially after meeting her friend Dylan, and our very lucrative cocaine-titties.

I wonder...

But I had been scared of everything... until I lost Selma.

What about...

Loosing someone you love, can make you feel like there is nothing left to lose, accept yourself.

Curiously enough, the loss of Selma, and the awful stabbing sensation of regret, made me feel dangerously invincible. The pain of it all was so immense, that there was no way I could ever imagine anything else hurting that much, or being that bad.

I don't care what happens anymore.

I felt reckless, and fearless.

I felt like...

...what would Selma do?

YOU CAN GET HAPPY AT THE BODEGA

33

Maria: So my mom used to tell me that grief makes us see our-selves, and those we love, more clearly.... but it sounded way more beautiful in Spanish.

I laugh.

Me: Yeah, I bet.

Maria gets up to get the bottle of Malbec she had opened the night before, and pours us each a glass.

Maria: You know... you don't talk about Selma much.

Me: Yeah... you're right... I don't.

Maria walks my glass of Malbec over to me.

Maria: Why not?

Me: I don't know. I guess I sort of wait for people to ask me about her, but no one ever does. Ever. I think they're all too scared to ask me...or something. I don't know, I think people are scared to talk about her... you know... like how she died.

It's quiet for a moment.

Maria: Well I'm okay talking about her, and it.

Me: I know you are.

I lean over, kiss Maria on her head, and she smiles at me, while holding up her glass for a toast.

Maria: To Selma.

Me: To Selma.

We cheers, and take a sip.

Maria: Hey, so if it weren't for Selma, you would've never stripped?

Me: That's correct.

Maria: I love that. It actually makes perfect sense too. It's so Selma.

So Selma.

I catch myself smiling as an image of Selma comes to mind. She's standing blissfully in front of the bodega at 4:00 AM, smoking her cigarette, wearing her vintage red bottoms, and pumping gas into her one of a kind, vintage Mercedes car... who she had once named Gertrude.

Me: So very Selma.

LESSONS FROM THE CLUB

34

First Lesson: Confidence

The very first time I ever stripped at the club, was the very first time I actually had to wipe the sweat off of my forehead, before going on stage.

Holy shit.

From the moment I entered The Dollhouse, it was clear that it wasn't going to be about how good I could dance (something I was use to relying on for confidence). This was going to be about how I looked... completely naked.

Shit.

I felt a wave of anxiety that I had only heard about.

Is this stage fright?

DJ: Victoria to the stage.

Fuck, that's me.

I wiped off the beads of sweat, and walked toward the stage.

My heart won't stop racing!

Then the first song started to play.

It was a techno version of a Journey song.

Shit.

There I was, trying not to look nervous, standing in disguise as 'Victoria'... wearing black seven-inch thigh-high vinyl stilettos, a neon-pink mesh mini-dress, and a diamond-studded black stripper-thong (the special one with clips on the side that made it easy to snap on, and off).

I hope those guys by the stage will like me.

All I could think about was getting their approval.

What if they boo me, like the boys from high-school?

It was the most intrusive thought I couldn't control.

I won't be enough.

I give away my power to total strangers, just like my time.

Are they going to make me feel worthless?

Am I worthless?

As I made my way toward the pole, I looked around the stage, and noticed all the different types of people looking at me. They weren't really eager, or excited. Their looks reminded me more of the judges at my dance competitions (as a kid), or the weird men who smoked in front of the fabric store (from when I was in high-school).

Shit.

I could feel more sweat beads starting to formulate.

My makeup.

I reached up for the pole with my right arm, and tried to remind myself that I was a trained dancer, and a hell of a performer. I tried to tell myself it would be just like go-go dancing at The Lounge back in college, even though I very much knew THIS would be nothing like THAT.

Try to breathe.

I leaned away from the pole, and started to walk in a slow circle, letting my head drop over to the side.

What do they think of me?

Then I hooked my ankle on the pole, fell into a soft spin, dropped to a split, and threw my head back (allowing my hair to fly back, out of my face).

Are they looking at me?

Do they want me?

How much will they pay me?

I caught a glance of one of the men staring at me, with a soft smile on his face. In his right hand was a cold beer, and in his left, a five dollar bill.

I think he wants me.

I took a step off the pole, and toward him. He tossed the five onto the stage, and put his beer down to reach for his wallet... then he pulled out a twenty dollar bill, and threw it onto the stage, for me. So I moved toward him.

Don't stop... believing...

Somewhere between Journey, and focusing on the twenty, I noticed I had stopped wondering, or even worrying about, what he, or anyone, was thinking of me. Instead, my thoughts were flooded with my new sense of power. A force so loud, that it drowned out the noise of worthlessness that once filled my head.

He definitely wants to give me all his money.

The intensity sent a shock wave through my body, the type that made me feel as though my legs were power titans, and my thighs, they were shields from shame. The jiggle in my ass was shaking to repel any bullets of booing, and best of all, I felt tall.

He's not so big.

It felt like I grew the actual seven-inches of my stilettos.

Looking down at you from up here, doesn't make me feel so small.

There was something about being on stage and standing (actually towering) over a man, in my seven-inch stilettos, and him, down in a chair, that made me feel invincible. It was about more than taking his money, it was freedom.

I feel like Charlie.

It was overwhelming me with a charge of energy, in a way even I was taken back by. I couldn't believe how bold, and strong I felt. Every empowering step I took toward him presented a shift in our dynamic, a shift I had not yet experienced with a man.

Just like Selma said.

Instead of fear filling my body, and taking my breath hostage, I felt calm. I felt confident, and I could breathe. I felt complete control, even while his bizarre gaze scanned my entire body.

I think I like this.

My power was larger than his.

I'm not scared of him.

I'm not scared of him, at all.

Perspective shifts more then just your perspective.

From his seat, he looked up toward the stage, and stared at me as if I had him in a trance (and I wanted to keep him that way).

I've never had this kind of high before.

I put my weight into every step I took in his direction (so to exaggerate my hips), and stared him right in his eyes… which made him succumb to me even more.

I know exactly what to do.

Then while keeping his eye contact, I slowly let my dress slip off my body, and drop down to my knees.

I bet I can figure out what he likes.

He pulled out another twenty dollar bill, and I crawled toward him exactly like Nomi did in "Showgirls". Just like I had imagined Selma did, when she was a stripper.

I bet he likes it.

Then, while letting him put his twenty into the top of my right thigh-high boot, I noticed out of the corner of my eye, another man, with an even larger bill in his hand.

A fifty dollar bill.

I want to do it to him too.

I took my money, and crawled over to him.

This is exhilarating.

It's not exploitation when you're the one in power.

It was a tangible reward for feeling something I had not felt in the presence of men, or anyone for that matter.

This must be confidence.

Second Lesson: Self-Love

In my first year working at the club, I had gotten pretty good at dancing on the pole, and selling lap-dances. All thanks to working three days a week, and some of the other strippers' assistance.

This isn't bad.

Overall, my confidence in performing as 'Victoria' had really improved, and it had even improved outside of the club... as me, as Layla.

I walk taller now. I don't apologize for my presence.

Maybe Selma was onto something...

Though, working at The Dollhouse, a place that demanded you stand in your own power, had made it unbearably clear that I didn't have even an ounce of self-love.

Is that not the same as confidence?

And it was a swift awakening, over the course of a few months, that made my unbearable truth painfully known to me.

Do they even like me?

Do I even like me?

My Painfully Swift Awakening:

It was the first day of March, and a crude customer on a power trip leaned over, and asked me (with an authoritative tone):

"Don't you love yourself?"

I don't know. Do I?

Then a month after that, the wife of one of my new customer's unexpectedly appeared, and said to my face, loud enough for everyone to hear over the music:

"Who could ever love you?"

I don't know. Who?

Finally by May, at a friend's baby-shower, another pseudo friend (who didn't know I was a stripper) said (out-loud), to everyone (including me):

"Strippers are disgusting... they're so dirty!"

Are they? Am I?

Everyone else's opinion is louder than my own.

For the rest of that summer, I walked around (in and out of the club) feeling defeated, embarrassed, and ashamed.

Stop!

It was clear that all my self-hate had become amplified, and all the shit I carried around before ever working as a stripper, was now becoming deafening.

Make it stop.

I hated myself more than ever before, and not because I was a stripper, but because now I couldn't pretend my self-hatred wasn't real. My lack of self-love was so present, that I couldn't separate people's hatred for strippers, from their hatred of me... or from my own hatred for myself.

Please make it stop.

No matter where I was, I couldn't escape it...

I don't love me.

I want someone else to do it for me.

In a moment of quiet desperation, I could hear loud and clear that I was waiting for anyone to love me.

* *

In the end, working as a stripper didn't heal my inability to love myself, not quite like it sparked the start of a cure for my lack of confidence. But it did give me the opportunity to at least start trying... a little bit.

Fucking people.

Actually, I had a few chances to try.

Assholes.

It would be when an angry self-loating customer asked me (again) if I really loved myself, or when I heard a cruel joke (again) about a stripper in a movie, at a party, or out at dinner with a (supposed) friend.

It's just a fucking job!

Every one of those moments gave me the opportunity to learn how to actively make a choice to own who I was.

She is NOT my friend.

They each gave me a chance to be proud of me, and love me just enough to get me through that one moment of their projected, privileged shaming.

They're just a bully.

Actually, working as a stripper helped me to at least figure out how to not make their bullshit, my bullshit. And how to start loving myself, just enough to hear the voice inside my own head, finally say:

Fuck 'em.

Third Lesson: Boundaries

I had come to understand that a sex-worker could be categorized under a plethora of options.

Strippers - Prostitutes - Live streamers - Porn Actress's - Friends who get paid by friends to do lines of cocaine of their titties - Sugar Babies - Dominatrix's - Foot Models

All of these people, and job titles, are people who monetarily capitalize on the art of seduction, and/or sexual satisfaction, by skillfully fulfilling the desires of a focused target market, with their said skills.

It's a job.

They specifically get paid, a specific amount of money, for a specific service they have consented to without force, or deceit. Also, sex-workers keep all of their money earned in a day; and during the time the service is being performed, the sex-worker is in control, and has full ownership over their entire body, the entire time.

What's control?

Those last points are crucial, because the difference between the sex-worker who has consented, and one who has not... is that, the one who has not, is clearly being raped, or assaulted. And someone who isn't keeping the money their making after their sex-work, is clearly being sex-trafficked.

There is obviously a difference.

Obviously.

Actually, to further distinguish the two, quite a few sex-workers tend to excel in creating, and establishing strong boundaries that prioritize their own worth, and safety. Therefore, they often tend to be capable of drawing very clear lines between consent, and assault.

Protecting yourself requires you to know your value.

Though not all sex-workers posses this ability.

We definitely do not.

And I was one that definitely did not.

What is my worth?

Just like with my confidence, and inability to love myself, the club had made it impossible to deny that I was clearly lacking the ability to create, and set boundaries.

What is a boundary?

Why can't I be like Esmerelda?

* *

Esmerelda was a stripper who walked like a queen, both in, and out of the club.

She floats.

Out of the club, she walked with her head held high, unapologetic, and aware. She always held the door open for someone else, barely wore any makeup, and almost always paid for breakfast after work. I didn't know much about her family, or home life (I think she wanted it that way), but the time I did spend with her was impactful. Esme was someone whose heart I could feel, even by spending just two minutes with her.

She's like Selma.

In the club, Esmerelda walked with her head held even higher. She was popular with customers, she held a good conversation, had regulars, wore lots of makeup, smelled like candy, and smiled all of the time.

Everyone wants her.

Yet a lot of the strippers assumed she was so popular with her customers, because she was having sex with them. That was until two infamous incidences occurred, where Esme proved everyone wrong... without even trying.

Fucking Esmerelda.

The Two Infamous Incidents:

The first, was the time my friend Trina and I went to give a doubles-dance, in the booth next to Esmerelda's.

There she is.

And because of an old crack in the mirror, and a new tear in the curtains, Trina and I (while grinding on each other), were able to see Esmerelda, in the booth next to ours.

I can't believe it.

For all eight songs (while Trina and I danced out every wet-dream fantasy, our customer ever had)...Esme (ever so comfortably), sat topless, sipped on her drink, and talked.

They're really just...sitting there.

For all eight songs, all they did was talk.

She just made as much money as I did!

That was it.

Just sat there!

Trina and I could not believe it. So as soon as our dou-bles-dance ended, Trina (known for knowing), went straight to the locker-room (intensely impressed with Esmerelda), and told every-one what she saw.

Trina: Hey! Esmerelda gets paid to sit and talk! Sit and talk! Okay! Ladies! No no no! We need to step up our talking game! That girl had that man pay-ing her-to-talk!

A few minutes after that, Esme walked into the locker-room, and everyone instantly started clapping for her.

Wow.

And that was the beginning of the end of the rumor.

I wonder what they talked about…

The second time she killed her own rumor, we all saw it hap-pen. It was during a very slow day-shift, and everyone was on the main floor, while Esmerelda was giving a floor-dance to the one cos-tumer in the whole club.

This place is dead.

Esme was standing over him, and rubbing her long red nails, through his long blonde hair. Then, out of nowhere, she stood up, and slapped the shit out of him.

Esmerelda: Get out! Now!

Customer: Fuck you, you cunt!

But then Esmerelda slammed her sparkling, cherry-red, eight-inch stiletto onto the top of his left thigh… just inches away from his penis, and said:

"Say it again you dick-dumb piece of shit! I dare you."

Fuck!

What'd he do?

We later found out (again, thanks to Trina) that the crude customer tried to stick his fingers up Esmerelda's vagina (which wasn't allowed). So, she slammed her stiletto onto his dick, and said what she said.

Damn.

Security, and the shift manager, walked the dick-dumb customer out right after that, no questions asked.

She just...

... did that.

* *

I, on the other hand, couldn't demand my worth the way Esme could. For me, when a customer tried to move past my panties, I'd let them. Not because I wanted them to, it was just... I didn't know how to say no.

I can't speak.

I would keep performing, float away, and let them in.

I can't move.

I sometimes feel like a windup doll, who's batteries are almost always dying, but no one cares if I'm dead.

One time, with this one customer, while they pushed their fingers inside me (without asking), I just let my body go numb, and sang out loud in my head.

Don't go chasing...

Then they pulled their fingers back into their mouth.

Waterfalls...

And licked them while looking me right in my eyes.

Did they expect that?

After work, all I could think about was getting clean.

I feel dirty.

I got home, and ran straight into my shower.

I feel so fucking dirty!

I didn't even take my clothes off.

Get it off me!

I turned on the water, grabbed the soap, and shuffled my things off into the tub. I just kept scrubbing and rinsing, over, and over again.

I still don't feel clean!

I smoked a bowl, ate nothing, and laid wide awake in my bed, trying to forget anything had happened.

I hate them.

It wasn't working.

I hate myself.

Over and over, my mind kept racing.

I let them....

It had become clear to me that I wasn't safe.

... I let them.

And even clearer that I couldn't trust...

...me.

SELF-LOVE AND
LAST BITES

35

I take another sip of wine, and another deep breath.

Maria: Wait, when's the last time you stripped?

Me: I haven't since … like six or seven months ago.

Maia: Why'd you stop? Not make enough money?

Me: No!

We laugh.

Maria: Then why not?

Me: Well… I realized I had no boundaries, and couldn't protect myself… at least not the way I wanted to.

Maria: Not like Esmerrrrrrrrrelda!

We giggle, and Maria starts to braid my hair, as I slip my head down onto her lap to relax.

Me: Yeah… Esme…she has her shit together. Like… I'm sure she's had her share of shit too. We all do. But it seems like whatever her shit is from the past, it definitely doesn't run her present… or future. It's like she's free from it all.

Maria: I bet my money Esmerelda has a therapist.

Me: But maybe she doesn't?

Maria finishes the long, loose braid she twisted into my hair, and wraps the red hair-tie she'd been wearing on her wrist all night.

Maria: Bueno! Believe me Layla... she does.

Me: I wonder...

Maria: Or did... or does.

Me: You're probably right.

Maria: I am.

I reach for the last of the pad-thai.

Maria: You better save me that last bite.

I wink at Maria.

Me: Never.

Maria lights up the joint, passes it to me, and I pass her the last of the pad-thai... only for her to pass it back to me.

Maria: Aye! I love you too.

LIE TO ME

36

The impulse to stop lying to myself, and everyone else, was starting to make itself known to me, and it felt shockingly strange (and nearly impossible) to navigate.

I don't want to pretend anymore.

But learning not to lie, at least for me, would be harder than learning a new language.

How do I tell the truth?

* *

The types of lies I had been living ranged from small, to large. On the smaller scale, I would lie when a friend would ask me a simple question, like:

"Have you tried meditating?"

And I would be like:

"Yeah I have! It's great."

But then in my head, I would be like:

My nervous system doesn't respond to calm, and why the fuck does yours?

Yet instead I would say:

"I love meditating. Let's do it together."

Why I'd just say that?

On a grander scale (with a higher risk of self-harm), the lying would happen while having sex.

Tell them you don't like it.

Layla! Tell them you don't like it!

No matter who I was having sex with, in these situations, I said, and did whatever it took to please them.

Whatever you want.

And it wasn't as simple as saying it would only happen with men, so-to-speak. The truth was, no matter who I was having sex with, I could not feel empowered enough to speak up for my needs, or my body.

Ouch!

Her nails are hurting me.

It had become so normalized to me, that in the moments I would do it, I couldn't even recognize it as a thing I was even doing.

I don't trust myself, with myself.

But the impulse itself, to really stop lying (for the sake of people-pleasing), pronounced itself to me in one of my most memorable, short-lived relationships. It was a classic doomed-dalliance, one that really echoed the sentiment of like-attracts-like.

My Doomed Dalliance:

One night, while filling my car up at a gas station, I was robbed.

Shit.

Apparently, when I got out to pump the gas, I forgot to lock the car. And while twisting off the cap, a man opened my passenger door, grabbed my bag, and ran off.

Shit!

But I didn't even know it had happened.

Not until this other man ran over to ask if I was okay.

Me: Yeah I'm fine. Why?... who are you?

Him: That guy just stole your bag! He just opened the door, took it, and ran!

Me: Oh shit! That's my dance bag!

Him: Your what?

Me: My dance bag.

He laughed.

Is he making fun of me?

In an unexpected twist of the expected (the expected being me freezing up, or running away), I boldly spoke out.

Me: Don't laugh at me! That's my whole fucking job in that bag! It's like all my shoes. Like six fucking expensive pairs of shoes. And my foam roller. My best foam roller! My knee brace. My fucking tape! Do you know how much KT tape costs? Per roll! Damn it! My favorite fucking sweatpants from college! Motherfucker!

I can't afford to replace all that shit.

Shit!

Him: Sorry I laughed at you.

Me: Whatever.

Why won't this guy just leave me alone?

Him: Well I'm Mark... are you, I mean, if you're not busy right now, can I buy you a drink across the street...that's where I was, when I saw that guy steal your bag.... from the window over there... I could help you file an insurance claim on your dance bag?

Me: Seriously? You're still making fun of me?

Then he smiled, apologized for patronizing me (again), started to walk back across the street, and finally... he stopped to look back, to see if I had changed my mind.

Nice smile.

It was the kind of smile, that made me smile.

Fuck it... I'm thirsty.

* *

That one unexpected date with Mark, across the street, turned into five more dates, over the next month.

One lunch - One drinks - Three dinners - No sex

I wasn't really looking for sex, or anyone when I met Mark. But he came out of nowhere, made me mad, then made me smile, and I kind of just wanted to keep smiling.

I need this right now.

* *

During those first five dates, I found out that Mark was seven years older than me, he did something in tech, he liked vintage cars, riding motorcycles, and he liked to talk (a lot) about his vintage cars, and motorcycles.

I don't really like him... but I don't really NOT like him.

Also during those five dates, I requested we arrive separately, just in case I ever needed to make a swift exit.

He really loves his cars.

Every time, I'd arrive (almost) on time, in my hunter-green SUV, while Mark had shown up early (all five times), and waiting at a table, set for two.

He's super punctual.

And... it always was nice. Nice enough for me to never have to make a swift exit.

This is distracting enough.

Then at the end of each date, he'd walk me to my car.

This feels good.

* *

On our sixth date, we went to a small place that seated about twenty people, served delicious homemade Italian food, and some of the best pasta I had ever tasted.

Fuckin yum!

As usual, Mark arrived five minutes early, and good thing too, because the restaurant was packed with a very large family (one that included babies, grandparents, and three other couples).

It's packed!

While waiting, Mark had ordered us a bottle of Pinot Noir, and an appetizer of mozzarella sticks.

I should finally tell him I don't eat cheese.

Dating can be fun for anyone who isn't a people pleaser, or just generally insecure. For them... I bet it's a blast.

By dessert, we were onto our second bottle of wine, and third hour of laughter; which is when I noticed a striking woman, dressed in all white, with her phone in hand (standing behind Mark), and calmly taking a video of the two of us.

The restaurant is filming us on their live stream?

So I giggled.

Me: Hey, they think we're hot enough for their feed.

Him: What?

Mark turned around to see what I was referring to.

Shit!

The fuck?

Suddenly, Mark was taken back by the woman in white (way more than I was). In fact, he looked as though he had seen a ghost.

What is happening?

Next, Mark screamed out in terror:

"Holy shit!"

Holy shit!

Then a seemingly choreographed telenovela transpired, for everyone at the intimate restaurant to enjoy.

This feels like a horror movie.

The Tele-Novella / Horror Movie:

1.   Mark flew out of his chair, and turned toward the woman in white.

2.   The woman in white slapped Mark's left cheek, twice in a row, with her right hand.

3.   Mark grabbed the woman in white's hand, and stopped her from slapping him a third time.

4.   The woman in white screamed at Mark: "How could you do this!"

5.   The woman in white, looked back at me, and started recording me with her phone again, while screaming out: "Here's the whore! Here's the whore!"

6.   Mark pulled the phone out of the woman in white's hand, and pleaded: "Please! Please... calm down."

7. The woman in white said to Mark: "Fuck you," and slapped him a third time.

8. Mark tried to reach for the woman in white's arm, to try and take her outside.

9. Mark got the woman in white outside for a few seconds, which is where she slapped him a fourth time.

10. The woman in white stormed back in, and walked right up to me (again).

11. The woman in white screamed at me: "You whore! You're a whore! You're a slut! A cheap slut!"

12. Then the woman in white got a little closer to me, and screamed: "You won't get a penny!"

    What is she talking about?

    Wait.

    He's fucking married?

    That's his fucking wife!

13. Mark ran back in to try and make her leave (again).

14. They both went outside (again).

15. Everyone in the restaurant watched them yell at each other, while I coped silently by drinking more Pinot Noir.

    What the fuck is going on?

16. While Mark stayed inside, the woman in white stormed back in, this time with tears in her eyes.

17. The woman in white screamed at me, while she cried: "We're married!"

I can't believe he's her fucking husband.

18. The manager came out, and asked the woman in white (kindly) to leave.

19. The woman in white stormed to the doorway, stopped, turned, and yelled: "Fuck you, you slut! Whore!"

20. Everyone in the restaurant, including me, watched the woman in white jump into a fancy white car, and speed away for good.

    A Maserati? How much money do they actually have?

21. Everyone in the restaurant, including me, then watched Mark get into an equally fancy black car, and drive off after the woman in white.

    He drives a Lamborghini?

    I thought he liked vintage cars, and motorcycles!

    He never mentioned…

    … he never mentioned her!

22. Another woman, dressed in teal (with blonde hair), who had been sitting next to me all night (on her own date), leaned over and said to me: "You should be ashamed of yourself."

    I should?

23. I tried to tell the blonde woman in teal, that I never knew he was married, but she didn't care.

24. The blonde woman in teal sneered at me, turned to her date, and said: "Let's get out of here."

    Really?

25. Then the waiter brought me the check.

Really!

26.   While attempting to pay for the check, I realized Mark had left his expensive sunglasses, and phone on the table (but no cash for the check).

I can't afford this.

27.   I maxed out my credit card, and paid for our $242 check, chugged the rest of my wine, left his shit on the table, and walked out as fast as I could.

28.   I ran to my hunter-green SUV, got in, and instantly broke down crying.

What the fuck.

What the fuck?

What the fuck!

29.   I could see people from the restaurant watching me.

Please stop looking at me.

30.   While crying, I turned the car on, put the gear in reverse, and stepped on the gas to pull out as fast as I could.

Please stop.

31.   Mark decided to come back (for what I guess was to retrieve his expensive sunglasses, and cell phone).

32.   I hadn't realized Mark came back, because I was solely focused on leaving as quickly as possible. So to get away from the peering eyes, I stepped on the gas (harder than usual), and failed to see Mark driving back into the parking lot.

33.   While aggressively reversing out, I blindly crashed into his beloved Lamborghini.

34. To be specific, I was driving my not-low-at-all SUV, so I drove back, up, and over the front hood of his very low Lambo.

     Him!

35. I bursted into tears.

     I crashed into him?

36. Mark didn't get out of his car, and neither did I (I just kept crying, and trying to catch my breath).

     Why is he even here!

37. Then Mark put his Lamborghini in reverse, and slowly backed up and moved out of my way, so that I could leave in my hunter-green SUV... without ever saying a word.

                              * *

That night, Mark tried calling and texting me, but I didn't answer, or respond. He lied to me, and he had lied to his wife.

He's a liar.

But then I thought:

So am I.

Though I wasn't married, I too had been in a relationship with someone else at the time. Someone I had been with for about a year, but in the past few months, that person had stopped making me feel desired, seen or loved.

What's wrong with me?

Is it me... or is it them?

But instead of talking about it, I just pretended everything was okay, I lied to them, and sought out a distraction.

Everything is fine.

I don't need you to want me.

I lied to them, and myself.

Really...

Then I met Mark.

...everything is fine.

Then I lied to Mark, myself, and my girlfriend.

And then Mark lied to his wife, and to me.

And now somehow, I had lied to his wife, too.

So fucking messy.

All because I couldn't be honest with myself, or my girlfriend at the time.

Messy Layla!

Not that I blamed myself for Mark's lies.

That was his fucking fault.

But I still felt like I had been punished in public, for not being honest with myself.

I hate myself sometimes.

And I couldn't stop obsessing over all of it...the woman in white, Mark, the blonde woman in teal, my girlfriend.

What the fuck are you doing Layla?

It was the first time I had stopped to ask myself that.

Layla!... what are you doing?

It was a moment that felt like many mini-moments adding up to something grand. At least I was hoping so.

Fuck you Mark!

But fuck you Layla!... you lied, too.

I knew somehow this was one of those like-attracts-like moments, and I couldn't look away any longer.

I wish I was someone else.

The truth was I was scared, so I lied.

* *

The next morning, I blocked Mark's number.

Fuck Mark.

A week later, I finally broke up with my girlfreind.

I'm sorry I was such a coward.

About seven months later, I met Zane.

Being honest with myself was missing from my life, but I was lying to myself about it.

IT'S NOT YOU, IT'S ME

37

Maria: But Layla! Up and over the fucking hood of his Lambo?! Dios mio! Tu es in un telenovela, for real! Well shit! He deserved that little fender bender anyways.

I giggle.

Maria: Damn! All that drama made me have to pee!

I laugh some more.

Me: Go.

Maria gets up and heads to the bathroom, leaving the door open so we can continue talking.

Maria: So have you ever lied to me, Layla?

Me: Mmm... well okay, so like... I had sex with Sean again... but, when you asked me about him yesterday, I told you that I hadn't even talked to him.

Maria: Sean! You fucked him again?

Me: I mean...well that, right there... the way you say Sean, sends this shiver down my spine, and then it's like I was programmed to please you, so to avoid the jolt, I say what I think you want me to say. Which ends up being a lie. A lie like... I haven't even talked to Sean.

Maria: Well shit!

Me: The thing is, it really is me, and not you.

Maria smiles as she walks back in from the bathroom.

Maria: My favorite break up line.

Me: Accept in this case, it's true. It is me, and not you. I mean, I didn't lie because of what you would do, or what you would say, I lied because I'm scared to let you down.

Maria: Damn Layla, that's deep, and sad...

Maria walks over, and gives me a hug.

Me: Thank you.

Maria kisses me on my cheek, and lights up the joint.

Maria: So... Layla... you fucked Sean again?

I look up with a guilty smile, and lean in for a hug.

Me: You really want to know?

LET ME PUT A BABY IN YOU

38

It was a Tuesday night, and there I was, standing blank-faced in my kitchen, chugging my glass of Malbec in order to swallow my little white $69.99 Plan-B pill. A pill that came encapsulated in a plastic box, which the pharmacy cashier, Greg, had to unlock for me. And as I chugged my Malbec, along with the little white pill (handed to me by Greg), I couldn't help but do the math.

It's been five weeks since my abortion.

It had been exactly five weeks since I had shoved four little white pills up my vagina, so that my cervix could soften and dilate, which caused unbearable uterine contractions to push my pregnancy tissue out, and make me believe that I was going to die on the white-tiled floor of my bathroom.

I want to die.

I want to leave my body, and never come back.

I took another sip (big enough to finish the entire glass), and reminisced on the series of cathartic events, that had led up to my decision to not make a baby... and needing a Plan-B pill five weeks later.

A Series Of Cathartic Events:

FIRST: Pregnancy tests were used.

I remember I was playing one of my comfort albums, Fugees, "The Score," on Selma's old record player.

I miss her.

It was helping to create quite a perfect moment for me. One where the song "Ready or Not" would play, while I paced in my kitchen, gulping wine, and waiting for the first of six pregnancy tests, to reveal its results to me.

Fuck.

They all came up positive, too.

I'm Pregnant.

All six of them.

I'm fucking pregnant.

I remember the first of the six so vividly. Within seconds, I watched the bright white wand, turn from a blank stick, to one with two pink lines.

Double fucking pink lines!

Shit!

I hate pink.

Over the next twenty minutes, I sat on the edge of my bathtub, and watched six at-home pregnancy tests turn positive. Then in an unfortunately obvious epiphany, I took into account that my period was in fact, four weeks late.

I'm really fucking pregnant.

I felt light headed, my entire body felt weightless, like I was floating, and I couldn't feel my feet. Everything just felt... funny. Then my body began laughing, entirely beyond my control too. I actually laughed so hard, that even my face started to feel distorted. It was like I was having the most surreal realistic experience...one I could not run away from, or avoid.

This is actually happening.

I was going to have to make a choice, and one I was not prepared to have to make. It's not like anyone really teaches about it, or talks about it in a way that feels like it helps anyone out, in the sort of "here's how to do it way."

What the fuck am I going to do?

It was at that moment my laughter turned into tears.

I'm really fucking pregnant.

SECOND: I was broke, and the internet wasn't helping.

I didn't know how to tell anyone I was pregnant, when less than four months ago, I had just gotten divorced. And the guy I had unexpectedly gotten pregnant with, was not at all who I divorced.

It's Sean's.

Consequently, I expected judgment from everyone.

What will people think?

Though it's not because anyone said anything to me.

I just thought it.

I assumed it.

I anticipated it.

I made it real.

What will people say?

Is people pleasing a disease? If so, what's the cure?

What am I going to do?

At the time I got divorced/pregnant, I had no savings or extra cash, and there was no alimony in my divorce.

How am I going to pay for this?

Am I being punished?

So I simultaneously self-loathed, sat down in my favorite wooden kitchen chair, and I googled.

Affordable pregnancy options?

Free options for pregnancy help?

My simplistic, yet methodical search, produced a top result for a place that offered free pregnancy testing, with a sonogram, and options for the pregnancy.

Options included: Abortion - Adoption - Keeping it

I feel so disoriented.

With fear racing through my body, I clicked on the link.

I mean, it's free.

People want to help vulnerable people, right?

* *

Unfortunately for me, the so called "free sanctuary for women" was one of those pro-life clinics, disguised as a pro-choice clinic...which was incredibly terrifying to discover.

The fuck?

Upon my arrival to the hidden-house-of-horror, I first filled out an intake form; which in retrospect was bizarre, because of questions like:

"Do you know who the father is?"

"What is your religion?"

"Are you considering abortion? If so, why?"

I've never done this before.

Then, after filling out the unexpectedly personal form, I was taken into a small room, with a brown leather couch, and walls decorated with photos of various fetuses. All the while, two women dressed in everyday clothing (i.e. NOT nurses), tried to tell me why I needed to keep the baby, or put it up for adoption.

I thought you were going to help me.

Finally, after an impromptu screaming match (between myself, and the two pretend nurses), I ended up escaping the pro-life clinic, by having to shove one of them out of my way, and run past two different doors. Two doors which I realized had been locked behind me.

What the...

They locked me in here?

I ran away from the clinic as fast as I could, all the way until I was in my car, with the doors shut, and locked.

They locked me in.

Then I just broke down, and let myself cry.

What just happened?

Do I... can I call the cops? ...What would I say?

I don't even want to tell anyone that I...that...

I definitely want an abortion.

THIRD: I began protecting myself, and I didn't tell anyone.

Sean and I had been friends since middle school, and ran into each other at a mutual friend's birthday party; where we discovered we had at least one thing in common.

The thing: divorce

I've had a kind of crush on him since school.

So... maybe?

I mean... maybe.

I wondered if it was possible that Sean was thinking the same thing.

What was that look?

I liked that look.

Apparently he did think it, and decided to make it known by asking me if he could kiss me, while we were waiting for our drinks at the bar.

Did he actually just ask me that?

Nothing like David.

I was taken back that an extremely handsome man, would even stop to ask this question. For me, a mere 'Miami Girl,' it had been my experience that men that good looking, often walk around assuming, and privileged.

They don't ask, they take.

He is sexy.

It was that question, that moment of asking for my consent (ontop of the tequila, and my broken post-divorced heart), that made me extremely wet, determined, and bold.

Me: So do you at all, want to um... I don't know, like go into one of the extra guest rooms, and like... have sex?

Did I just say that?

Sean stared at me, and for a moment I couldn't tell if he was figuring out a witty answer, or just figuring out a way to back out.

Shit! Did I...

But to my honest surprise, he grabbed the bottle of tequila from the bar (and my hand), then guided me up the stairs into one of the empty guest bedrooms.

Neither one of us chose self-protection that night.

* *

That night (the one where Sean and I rendezvoused with tequila, and unprotected orgasms), was exactly twenty-two days after my five year marriage ended, and about three months after Sean's divorce.

This feels better than hurting.

Suffice to say, after that one night, neither he, or I, were in a place to nurture any sort of relationship. So we simply texted each other... as minimally as possible.

Sean's text: How ru?

My text: I'm ok. How ru?

Sean's text: I'm cool

My text: cool

* *

Weeks then went by without me thinking about Sean.

Fuck.

That was, until I saw double pink lines.

I hate pink.

But for me, my decision on how to handle the pregnancy had nothing to do with him, or our casual coping situation. Instead, for me, my decision to abort the pregnancy was based on my realization that I:

... don't want a baby.

Not like this.

Not now.

Maybe not ever.

* *

I had finally come to the conclusion not to tell Sean, or anyone else for that matter. I simply didn't want to take the chance that anyone would try to tell me what to do, or shame me for what I wanted to do.

I care too much about what other people care about.

Plus, I had already felt the unforgettable pressure of delusional cos-playing nurses.

What do I want?

It was a choice I needed to be sure of, and clear about.

Listening to myself is deafening.

It was a choice only I'd have to live with.

If I tell anyone... I'll let them tell me what to do.

And I'll want them to.

So I won't.

FOURTH: Florida made everything a little harder.

It so happened that I got pregnant in the state of Florida, a state that borders other southern states. States that work diligently to keep abortion-bans banning. Therefore, abortions were in high demand, and not easy to schedule.

Why won't anyone answer the phone?

Why can't I just book this online!

But finally, after two full days of calling, I got through to someone who could help me.

She sounds so tired.

I had gotten someone on the line, who I could tell had been on the phone as long as I had.

Can I tell her I'm scared?

Me: Hi, I'm pregnant, and I need an abortion.

I hope she can help.

The restless woman on the phone told me that Florida's Planned Parenthood's only offered surgical abortions, and the first availability they had, was at a clinic... six hours away from Miami.

Their earliest availability: five fucking weeks

I think I'm eight weeks pregnant.

I hung up the phone abruptly, and tried a second google search.

I can't wait that long.

This time I typed in: Gyno in Miami that offers abortions

There was one.

Literally, actually... just one.

Fucking why though?

So I called the one, and thankfully, a seemingly patient receptionist answered.

Receptionist: We can get you in next Tuesday morning. Does that work for you? And do you have insurance?

Me: Yeah I can come Tuesday. No, I do not have any insurance... of like, any kind.

Who has insurance?

Then the empathetic receptionist told me the total cost for everything, would include:

1) medical pregnancy test / appointment... $200

2) sonogram to confirm pregnancy gestation... $300

3) the abortion itself... $800

Shit!

I need money now.

Why is this is so expensive?

I'm going to have to...

Shit.

I fearlessly took the Tuesday appointment, and decided I'd get the money I needed, by working at the club, for the next five days in a row.

I don't know what else to do.

After five highly motivated days, I was able to make $3,510 (after tip-outs, etc.) ... which would be enough to cover the cost of my unplanned needs.

The cost of unprotected sex, is more expensive for she, then it is for he.

* *

I arrived at my appointment completely nervous, tense, and ready to pay in full.

I just want this to be over.

After a twenty minute wait, I was taken into the back, and asked to pee into a cup; where the medical test (which seemed exactly like my at-home test) showed that I was in fact pregnant.

Well I already knew that.

Then it took fifteen minutes, for the sonogram to confirm that I was eight weeks pregnant.

I thought so.

Finally the gynecologist smiled gently at me, and sat down to discuss the two ways she could offer me support.

Okay?

1) If I decided to keep it, there were options. Options such as government, and non-profit support for state medicare for single

moms, and organizations that specialized in adoption, if I wanted to go that route.

or

2) If I decided abortion, there was one. It was a medical abortion, and that was it, because it was illegal for her to perform a surgical abortion (even though she was a board certified surgeon). Legally, in Florida, she could only offer me the one with the pills... which of course wasn't covered by any sort of government, or insurance aid.

... *fuck.*

Why does this feel like a punishment?

I told her I absolutely wanted the abortion.

Mrs. Gynecologist: Okay.

Immediately she called in the nurse, who handed me the first white pill (the one that would stop the pregnancy hormone from producing). Then the doctor told me that in three days, I was to take the other four pills (the ones that would terminate, and shed the pregnancy). And a week after that, I would have to be back in for a follow-up appointment... to confirm that it worked.

Mrs. Gynecologist: There's a small percentage that it might not work, and in that case we'd have to try again.

Seriously?

Really?

Fuck me.

FIFTH: Four white pills went up my vagina.

Three days after taking the first pill at the doctors office, I stood in my bathroom, spread my legs, and pulled the lips of my vagina apart...just like if I was going to masturbate. Only this time, on my index finger, were four pills that were about to perform a cata-strophic miracle, in just twenty to thirty minutes.

This hurts so fucking bad!

* *

Six hours later, I wanted to give up. The pain, the nausea, the fever... it had all become too close to being too much to handle.

You can do this Layla.

Come on! You can do fucking this!

Wait! What the fuck is coming out of me?

Thankfully, I'm a woman, so I had the strength to survive the feeling of my body ripping to shreds.

Finally, after a total of eight hours, the nearly deadly cramping had lightened to a heavy period cramp.

I can't take it anymore.

The fever, and nausea would subside next. But only because I had an emergency prescription called in, and delivered to alle-viate the vomiting (which, really was only yellow mucus, because there was nothing left in me to throw up).

It's everywhere.

My vomit, cervix tissue, and sand-dollar sized blood clots were on the floor, in two buckets, and all over the toilet.

It smelled like trauma.

After I barely crawled into the bathtub, I just sat there wide eyed, looking at pieces of myself all over the white tiled floor.

What just happened?

I grabbed my sponge, dipped it in the water, and washed off the rest of the bile, and bloody tissue from my body. Then, for the third most indelible time during the pregnancy, I cried out loud.

I want my mom.

I couldn't believe the amount of pain (both physically and mentally), that I had just endured.

I'm so tired.

Those eight brutal hours, were eight hours that my body couldn't wait to forget as fast as possible.

I'm going to pass out.

I had never been so exhausted.

SIXTH: Greg really pissed me off, a lot.

Five weeks after my abortion, I found myself having sex with Sean, again.

It's been five weeks?

Five weeks after I had an abortion (one I barely could afford, or that Sean even knew about), there I was, doing it all over again... without protection, with the same guy.

Is this... what I want?

To clarify, I absolutely did want to be having sex with Sean again. That wasn't the question, or my pending doubt.

I just want to feel good.

There was no denying that I liked sex with Sean.

I miss Zane.

With Sean, I didn't have to think about how much I missed Zane, our divorce, or Selma.

I just want to feel better.

Wait... do I deserve to feel...good?

It's hard to receive pleasure, when your body has known so much shame.

But as I said, the detail of having sex with Sean, again, just weeks after my abortion, was not what had me feeling guilty. What was ailing me, was that I had realized (for the second time), neither of us stopped to use a condom.

Shit! I don't want to get pregnant... like this!

Again!

Just say stop, say you changed your mind.

But this feels good...

I just wanna feel good... everything feels so bad.

Can I tell him to stop now?

He's already inside of me.

Just say stop.

But in that moment, I didn't know how.

Just say it.

I couldn't.

Just say it!

So I didn't.

Fuck.

Then Sean pulled out, and came all over my lower belly.

Just like he did, when I got pregnant.

Shit. I need a Plan-B.

Fuck. Why I didn't just get one the first time.

* *

I decided to face Greg (the cashier), who would unlock my Plan-B, while checking me out (in more ways than one).

Fuck Greg.

I wanted to kick Greg in his face.

Stupid fucking face.

I had so much pent up anger, anxiety, and fear stirring in me, and Greg was making it all feel amplified.

I fucking hate him, and his fucking name tag.

G-R-E-G. I fucking hate Greg!

* *

That night, when I got home with my vagina life-jacket, I was undoubtedly fueled by the anger I felt for Greg, and everything else racing through my mind.

Fuck everyone!

So I leaned in, and allowed it to drive me to my victory.

No one can tell me what to do!

I stood pissed off in my kitchen, and very motivated.

Who the fuck does everyone think they are!

I ambitiously gulped my wine, and little white pill, fought off any lingering shame by blasting Salt-N-Pepa's "None of Your Business, " on Selma's vintage record player; and then, as proud as ever, I went to bed... and I slept like a baby.

It's none of your business!

COOKIES ARE
FOR COPING

39

Maria: Oh we love our vagina lifejackets!

Maria and I laugh, as she heads to her bedroom to change out of her yellow sun-dress, and into an old pair of black sweat-pants, with a royal blue oversized YMCA t-shirt. Then on her way back in from the bedroom, she brings me a cozy blanket, and some Reese's peanut-butter cups she had stored in her freezer.

Maria: Also, I understand why you didn't tell me about it until now.

Me: Really?

Maria: Absolutely, and I don't care. You don't owe me, or any-one, that part of you... not unless you want to share it. Like... only if and when you want.

Me: Thank you.

Maria: Thank you for trusting me.

Maria takes a bite of her peanut butter cup.

Maria: Meanwhile though...can I say! I hate how expensive Plan-B is. . . and fuck all the Greg's.

Me: Yeah, fuck the Greg's, and everything about pregnancy prevention being expensive as fuck!

Maria reaches for the joint, lights it up and takes a hit.

Me: I think it's because shaming women is so common, especially slut-shaming, so making it safe for women to be sexual would be the antithesis of all that shit.

Maria: And probably unacceptable to the motherfucking patriarchy.

She passes it to me.

Maria: It's like please see me as more than a thing of service, or a fucking baby incubator. I mean I did it, I incubated a baby, but it was my choice, and it's not the thing that defines me, or even makes me special... well, actually... it does kinda make me look down on some people, sometimes, I mean, when I'm riding on top! Hah!

We both laugh.

Maria: Hey you want some cookies? I know you do!

I giggle, as Maria walks to the kitchen, and yells out.

Maria: Hey! How cute is it that we met while getting cookies!

Me: Yeah, but Maria... like at a meeting for suicide loss!

Maria: Well Layla! Cookies are always cute! That's why they're at meetings for suicide loss... it's obviously very necessary!

Me: If only cookies cured depression.

A DEPRESSING
MEET CUTE

40

I remember reading this latin expression, which I found to be rather jolting.

Carpe diem.

Seize the day - Do it - Don't waste your time - Live now

It was written on a poster, inside the waiting room of an urgent care I had gone to for strep throat (a few months after my abortion). Under the phrase, was one lone penguin, standing at the edge of a cliff, and considering whether or not to jump.

It should jump.

While looking at the penguin, who was diligently deciding its own fate, the expression awakened something in me.

Carpe diem.

It wasn't the translation of the phrase, or the indecisive penguin, instead it was the brutal honesty of the sentiment itself.

Fucking penguin.

The meaning of the expression, and the insinuation of the penguin's ability to "seize the day," forced the gravity of my opaque depression right out of my carefully constructed blind spot.

I can't carpe diem.

I couldn't figure out if it was my unpacked baggage from the past, or some more recent life changing events.

Selma.

My divorce...

...the pandemic.

However, for the very first time, I wondered if...

Am I like Selma?

I had clearly become an expert at escaping, and dissociating from pain, and fear. Yet, I could not master the art of escaping my depression. I mean, I would get close to it, whenever I would dance, drink wine, have good sex, or anything else that provided me instant pleasure, and escapism. But sadly enough, it was only ever fleeting.

Pleasure over pain, please.

Before loosing Selma, I had never stopped to feel the full weight of my sadness.

Fucking carpe diem.

But now it was heavier than the anvil that came with learning of her suicide.

Fucking penguins!

I was suddenly very aware of myself, and not because I wanted to be.

I feel like I'm open on the surgeon's table, but I'm wide awake, and unable to move.

It was a lot.

This feels like too much.

But if I was being honest with myself...

I've always kind of felt like this.

It had always been hard for me to just be...happy.

I'm not even sure what that means.

Happy.

What does that feel like?

Even when I was a kid, I was more often scared, unsure, anxious, highly aware, and on alert.

Isn't that everyone?

However, every now and then, I could get happy for a moment, or two.

Playing dress up with my Grandma.

Rollerblading with Frida Garcia.

My parents swinging me in the air.

These things would bring me joy in the moment, but the moments were short lived, and I could never hold onto that joy for that long. It would happen, I would feel my whole body smile, and then within minutes (at most), the feeling would flee, and I would forget it ever even happened. But with dance, I could focus on something until I mastered it, and dance was hard to master, so it occupied my attention. Also with dance, I could learn how to take control of my body, and do powerful things with it.

I'm stronger than Eddie in dance.

Instead of feeling out of control, I felt like a superhero.

He can't touch me here.

Yet dance wouldn't be my solution to sadness.

Everything hurts.

* *

As an adult, it had become equally hard for me to pinpoint my own happiness.

Can you tell me what will?

At times, like when I was a kid, I'd come to discover things that gave me pleasure (which I took for happiness).

Hiking.

Concerts.

Dancing.

Listening to my headphones while riding a bike.

Sex (sometimes).

Is pleasure, and happiness the same thing?

Yet, like when I was a child, when the moment was over, and the experience induced happiness came to an end... I felt like a balloon deflating.

It never lasts.

Dance though... dance had always been a way for me to keep the balloon inflated, for a while.

I like the distraction.

At its best, dance was a steady, and sustained inflation of joy. The classes, rehearsals, productions, shows... all of it required me to put in eight hour, physically demanding days, and fill my head with tasks that I sincerely cared about.

Fix your arm, and get your leg higher.

Make it more interesting.

Make it perfect.

Breathe so you feel the movement!

But dance was beginning to loose its effect on me.

Everything from my past was catching up to me fast.

And I noticed the amount of time I could spend focused on my body, was becoming as fleeting as my happiness.

Everything in my present was catching up even faster.

Help me.

* *

A fear that had become bigger than my fear of losing my love for dance, was the fear of what everyone would think, if I told them how badly I was feeling.

I've never felt this low.

I didn't want to scare them, like Selma once scared me.

I can't.

So I kept it to myself.

I'll try the internet again.

My search: suicide help Miami

Whatever.

I clicked on the first thing that came up.

A meeting for suicide loss?

* *

With great hostility, I went there looking to poke holes in the theory that therapy of any kind (especially in the form of a group), could really do a thing for me.

Fuck this.

But then…

Who is that?

I saw Maria.

She dresses like Selma.

Maria stood there in a cropped lime-green button down, with vintage looking denim cargo pants, a purple Telfar purse, white slide heels, a perfect french mani/pedi, and light lavender hair pulled up into a tight bun with curls falling down over her forehead.

Maria: Hola, I'm Maria.

Maria shared with the group how she lost her dad to suicide, when she was eight.

Gun shot...

..like Selma.

And more recently, her sixteen year old brother accidentally took a small, but lethal dosage of fentanyl, when he thought he was getting molly, from a kid at his school.

Fuck.

Then, at the end of her group share, Maria opened up.

Maria: I don't know, I just feel like I wanna float away on a banana raft, with a fat-ass blunt, and my headphones blasting Betty Davis... "Nasty Gal," and be done.

Seriously, who is she?

I didn't know if it was her Selma-esque style, the dark humor, or the Betty Davis reference... but something made me walk right up to her.

I have to meet her.

Me: Hey. I'm Layla.

Maria: What's up? I'm Maria...Hey!...

She started to whisper.

Maria: Do you have any weed?

Me: Seriously?

Maria: Is that no?

Me: No. Yeah! Yeah I do. But why'd you ask me that? Do I look like I smoke weed?

Maria: Well... I mean... you are here, and it's fucking depressing here. Sometimes it's so depressing, I leave and go to the AA meeting down the hall, just to feel some hope. So if your not smoking weed... I mean... what are you taking? Or are you really here fully sober?

So Selma.

Me: No I'm not sober. I smoked a bowl before I walked in, and I picked up another eighth on my way here.

Maria: Amazing. I'll CashApp you. Where's your car?

Very Selma.

* *

As soon as we got to my car, Maria offered to roll a joint with her strawberry papers, and asked me to put some music on.

I wonder what music she likes to listen to.

I connected my phone, and a playlist started playing exactly where it had left off, midway through Amber Mark's "Lose My Cool".

I love this song.

As soon as the song came on, Maria belted out the lyrics, as if she had written them for Amber Mark herself. Then, as the rest of the song played, she finished rolling up and opened up to me, as if she'd known me her whole life.

She's so honest.

She told me she had once broken the windows of her ex-boyfriend's car, after she caught him cheating on her.

I wish I would've done that.

And that she sometimes steals blue nail polish, because it was her brother's favorite color.

I definitely get that.

Then, as I took a hit from her neatly rolled joint, I asked Maria how many of these meetings she had been to.

Maria: A lot girl!...a fucking lot. So like, my dad... he killed himself when I was eight, with the... well you already heard it. But that was like, over twenty years ago... but once I became a teen my mom got scared. I got really angry, and quiet, did a lot of drugs, started drinking, stealing... all of it. So she brought me to one of these...and I don't know... I just liked it. I liked how it calmed me, knowing I wasn't the only one who was fucked up. And they're everywhere, you know?... these meetings... you'd be surprised! I mean, back then, I was at groups for teens...but ANYWAYS!... I'm getting off track...so...sometimes, it hurts all over again, the same way it did when I was a kid, so I come to one of these, usually when I'm feeling heavy, like when I start to steal the blue nail polish... I come to this sad ass meeting, so I can be as broken as I feel, just like everyone else in the room... and talk about it. And I don't know! Sometimes, I will meet a 'you,' and end up smoking some very good weed... which! Thank you by the way!

I passed the joint to Maria, and sat in astonishment at how open, and vulnerable she was being with me.

Me: So you... actually make friends here?

Maria: No girl! I'm just kidding. You're the first. But you're cool. You have good taste in music, good taste in weed, I mean you seem sad as hell, but who isn't? Right?

I laughed.

Me: Right.

I was so relieved to meet her.

Maria: Now! Let me text my boyfriend, with his perfect penis, because mommy-dearest has a babysitter all night long! Hey!

Me: A perfect penis?

Maria: Yes! He has the perfect dick. You wanna see it?

Me: No!

We started to laugh.

Maria: Oh well I can't show you anyway's, because he didn't tell me that I could.

Permission for dick-pics? ...honestly.

Maria: I learned that consent shit in another group meeting I go to... when I started stealing blue polish... the group is for survivors of childhood sexual abuse.

Me: There's a meeting for that?

Maria: Yes ma'am! I told you! There's a meeting for everything. I mean, at first... I tried to go to the general sexual abuse one, but it was too triggering for me, because mine just happened to me four years ago. So in the one for children, like it happened to them way back then! And everyone is mostly an adult now, and their experiences sound nothing like mine. So it's better for me. Not for them.

I felt so close to her.

Me: What happened to you?

I can't believe I just asked her that.

Maria: Some asshole I met at a bar, put some shit in my drink one night, and basically kidnapped me. And then when I woke up, I was tied up, and he was fucking me... just like this actor I dated, but he didn't kidnap, or tie me up. He just fucked me in my sleep. But no lie, the entire FBI came to me, because this guy had done this to multiple women before! So I ended up even testifying against this guy, but like anonymously, but like still... I did, I testified.

A Depressing Meet Cute

Me: That really is amazing. I mean, what you did is amazing! Not that he raped you was amazing! I mean... that's the most bravest fucking thing I've ever heard.

Maybe I can tell her what happened to me.

Maria: Anything like that ever happen to you?

I MADE YOU
THIS PLAYLIST

41

The smoke cloud from all the weed laid flat on top of us, like a warm blanket of awakening, and truth.

Maria: Okay one, thank god we met before lock down, right! I mean, imagine if we would've met on zoom? Also... two, I love you, but I can-not, and will not, be your reason for living, or being happy! That's too much fucking pressure for me, so let's be clear about that. We both know how that ends, alright?

I take another hit, pass it back to Maria and assure her I agree.

Maria: So... You fucked Sean again?... Tell me!...How good was it?

I giggle.

Me: You're ridiculous.

Maria: No I know. But Layla. My love... from the way you described sex with him... girl, I'd probably pay to read that fifty-shades paper-back.

We laugh, I pass her the joint, and then throw the lighter at her.

Me: Shut up!

She lights up the joint.

Maria: I'm just saying! I'd read it, then watch the movie!

Then she throws the lighter back at me, and takes a hit.

Me: Stop it! It's not like that, he's not like that.

Maria: No?! Then what's it like Layla?

Me: I don't know... I just... I don't trust myself to fall for the right person. Like ever. I just... I always fall for people who don't love me the way I want them to. Or I blow it up.

Maria: I feel that.

Me: You don't trust yourself either?

Maria: No, I do. Now I do. But, I remember what it's like not to, and it sounds a lot like you, mi amor.

Maria giggles, and I snatch the joint from her in spite.

Me: Shut up. So then how? How did you learn to trust, and love yourself... like that much?

Maria: By staying single baby! For a while! I mean, you gotta be single... for at least a year! Like for one whole entire year, you need to be with just you. Just you in a full on relationship... with you!

Me: Fuck.

Maria: What?

Me: I haven't been single since the eight grade. I think. Yeah... I've like, always been with someone. Like Always.

Maria: Like always?

Me: Like always.

Maria lays down on the couch, I put down the joint, and lay my head back down onto her lap.

Maria: Well! I think you need to find out! Because that attachment shit, that needing to be with someone, like their a fucking drug, like you're dependent on their amor, that shit is gonna keep you in this cycle of mierda! For real!

I look up toward the ceiling, as if there's an answer waiting up there for me.

Maria: Layla! Hello! Look at me. Mira! Right now!

I look at Maria, right into her stoned, laser focused eyes.

Maria: Layla, all this shit about shaming yourself, and feeling guilty for how you've needed to just figure out your shit, the way you did it, like fuck it! You do you. Fuck everyone else! And you know, for the record, I don't think there's anything wrong with you, at all. And anyway's, I think we're all just programmed to shame ourselves unfortunately... at least, I think so. But yeah! Fuck everyone, and do you!

Me: Everyone?... Fuck everyone?

Maria: Well... okay so maybe don't fuck everyone Layla! Bueno mira! ... Unless you really want to.

Maria squints her eyes together, gets a giant smile on her face, and we both giggle.

ANOTHER NOIR SHADE OF LIGHT

42

I wake up in the middle of the night, terrified I'll let everyone down.

* *

It had been three days since I last spoke to Maria, due to the 'dark-nothing' that had (for the first time), creeped into my brain, taken over my body, and became utterly determined to keep me there.

Am I going to be like this forever?

I had finally hit my rock bottom, and I was glued to it.

I can't move.

I had been living everyday fearing the worst, and now it was stronger than ever, especially since many of my worst fears, had all recently come true.

Lose someone I love to suicide…

… and regret my last moment with them.

Get pregnant, while single, and have an abortion.

Realize that my waking dreams from when I was a little girl, are real-life nightmares.

Have to navigate a global pandemic…

… that will wipe away everyones way of living.

My partner will leave me, because I'm not good enough.

But it wasn't the things that happened to me, per-say…it was the why's, and why not's. To get specific, what glued me to the floor, what had tipped me all the way into the final abyss, was my most recent fear realized… the one documented on paper, and available for everyone to see, a-la public record: my failed marriage.

Why is this happening?

What did I do?

That was when the time bomb (the one that had been ticking inside of me since I was a little girl), went all the way off, and paralyzed me from the inside out.

Spending your whole life trying to swim, can make you want to sink.

What did I do wrong?

A TIME BEFORE YOU

43

Maria: Hey… wait! How did you, and Zane meet? By the time you and I met, you two were already getting divorced.

That's true, you never even met Zane, huh?

Maria: Nope.

Me: Strange.

Maria: Right?! And they were such a big part of you!

Me: Yeah…they really were.

I reach for the joint, and Maria reaches for the lighter.

Maria: I mean… I'm listening mi amor.

Maria passes me lighter, and I light up the joint, to pass it back to her. Then she lights it up, and takes a hit.

Maria: I'm still listening…

I lay my head back down on Maria's lap, and she passes me the joint for a hit.

I'M MADE OF GLASS

44

I met Zane in typical millennial fashion.

I can't believe we met on IG.

A friend of mine had sent me Zane's page, for a show I was choreographing. She knew I was looking for a painter to design the stage-set, and from what she saw, she thought our styles might blend. And she was right, Zane and I hit it off... we immediately blended.

I like how they think.

I slid right into their DM's.

My DM: Hi. I'm Layla.

Zane's DM: Hey. I'm Zane.

* *

For the next five years, Zane and I would experience that kind of love that was dependable, and electric.

I love you.

Do I deserve you?

I want to forget about everything else in this fucked up world, and just spend my time loving you.

Our love was beautiful, and filled with joy, and trust.

I'm okay.

Especially during sex.

I'm safe.

Then we did something I never imagined myself doing.

I want to marry you.

Our wedding was perfect, too. It was just the two of us (and our parents), in a small courtroom, on a Thursday.

I do.

Afterwards, we spent the weekend in an Airbnb that had a pool (and a hot tub); and we left our phones on airplane mode... the entire time.

This is perfect.

It was exactly what we wanted it to be.

I love you so much.

But without warning (and within a year), life came at us viciously, and without apology.

I don't understand.

Our fragmented past often comes into focus in the present. And when that happens... if not prepared, it can become nearly impossible to see the future.

Is it my fault?

My issues?

Why did it get so bad, so fast?

Life was testing us, and we were failing miserably. Neither of us yet knew how to be a partner, or even how to love each other (needless to say ourselves), through the worst of times... through a pandemic.

Who's to blame?

In the end, Zane asked for the divorce.

I'm to blame.

It was our last fight, and we never even kissed.

* *

In a matter of fifteen months, I had lost my best friend to suicide, survived a pandemic, gotten divorced, quickly had sex with Sean, eventually got pregnant, had my medical abortion, failed at fucking my way to happiness, and now months after that...

I'm so done.

I'm exhausted.

I'm so numb.

I've been numb.

While dazed off in my bathtub, and allowing my skin to shrivel up into a discolored raisin, I awakened to the feeling that my anger wasn't about Zane at all.

I hate myself.

I wasn't mad at them.

I really hate myself.

I was pissed off at me.

Fuck me.

It had taken weeks of me spent alone crying and drinking, followed by weeks spent fucking and crying (while drinking), that finally culminated in one fateful week, where I found out (while drinking), that the fucking had gotten me pregnant.

I really hate myself.

had become clear to me that Zane had done what we both needed to do, and it was painfully obvious when they said to me:

"You know we're not happy anymore."

I'm scared to admit it.

But they were right, we weren't happy anymore.

I don't want to admit it.

We were both depressed, angry, confused and frustrated with ourselves, each other, and the rest of the world... and we were taking it all out on the person we loved most.

Our balloon deflated.

It was over.

Are we over?

And then a daunting thought began haunting me.

I'm not lovable.

Which was accompanied by a parade of intrusive thoughts, that ambushed me, while I laid on the floor, weighted down, by my unquestionable depression.

How could Zane have ever loved me?

They were too good for me.

I'm too fucked up for them.

Are they happy now, because they aren't with me?

Was being with me, the thing that made them unhappy?

Do I make those I love unhappy?

Honestly... who could ever love me?

Low thoughts.

No one will ever love me.

I'm always ready and willing to suffer.

The shame filled thoughts, playing on repeat, started to get worse, and grew louder.

Please make it stop.

I can't take it anymore.

Make it stop!

Is this what happened to Selma?

Next, the tunnel vision came on quickly.

Nothing matters.

Within an hour, I was apathetically floating, and entirely lost in the abyss of nothingness.

I was steadily sinking into not giving a fuck.

It felt like all the energy I had left in me to keep on going, had passed empty, and my engine was about to turn all the way off.

I'm so tired.

Nothing, or no one matters.

Over time, I became so isolated, and consumed by my sadness, that I forgot how to consider the people I loved. It felt like the dullness of light was erasing everyone from my focus, and they were disappearing into the nothingness, along with the rest of me.

No one else understands.

No one understands me.

I've considered my erasure from this world with the ease of watching (what I have imagined to be) my final sunset.

* *

After that, I went on to spend an entire two (maybe three) days in bed.

I want to leave, and never come back.

While laying there, entirely awake, and completely unrested, I began thinking about all the ways in which I would want to die.

How can I painlessly leave, and never come back?

But my list was relatively short.

My list: a lot of pills

Pills won't hurt.

It had become clear that my daily battles with anxiety, depression, trauma, triggers, and a lack of self-love, were taking over my ability to believe that a better anything was possible.

I feel hopeless.

And I had become more exhausted than I'd ever been.

It doesn't go away.

I just wanted to go to sleep.

Forever.

So while hiding from the world in bed, I decided to text the few people in my phone that might know a random dealer for me. One who would sell me whatever I wanted, no questions asked, as long as I paid in full.

Who can I text?

I figured if I scrolled through my phone, I could get something within the hour.

Shit.

I need to turn my phone back on.

With the least amount of enthusiasm possible, I reached for my phone, which had been tucked under my pillow and turned off for the past two (maybe three) days.

I forgot.

I turned my phone back on, and texted Rodney (someone I barely knew, but who I'd met at one of Selma's parties, and someone who sold all the drugs, to everyone).

My text: need pills for sleeping - 20

Shit!

Fuck.

My phone had attempted to think for me.

Shit.

While typing in the "R" and the "O," my phone picked a 'top name' in my contacts.

Ro...

Yet, in my depressive (and determined) daze, I failed to even notice.

Fuck! Robby!

Not Rodney.

Shit.

Robby, my actual friend from high-school, called right away.

Fuck-shit.

At first, I didn't answer.

He'll keep calling if I don't answer.

He'll come over if I don't answer.

So after his third time calling, I finally answered.

Me: Hello?

Robby: Layla! What the fuck! Are you okay?

I considered I'd ease his mind, and tell him I was fine, just tired, and having trouble sleeping.

Robby: What the hell Layla?

Lie to him.

Me: I'm just tired. And haven't been able to sleep, so I was just... trying to find something to help me out. And I meant to text Rodney, but instead my phone texted...

Robby: Layla! You sound worse than tired Layla! What's going on? Do I need to come over? Max will watch the kids.

Me: No I'm fine.

Robby: I don't believe you.

Me: Really... I just need to sleep. I haven't slept.

All of the sudden, I started to forget what day it was, or even where I was. I knew I was talking to Robby, but I wasn't sure if it was real, or a dream. It was all starting to blur together.

Damn, Robby pants-ed me.

My mind had somehow wondered back to high-school.

Me: Hey Robby...

Robby: Yeah?

Me: Do you remember in high-school, when you pulled my pants open in front of everyone.

Robby: Layla! What are you talking about?! That's it! I'm coming over right now!

Me: Robby I'm fine. My mind is just like... skipping around.... because I'm tired. But no...do you? Do you remember?

Robby: Layla!

Me: I just...I was telling Maria about it a few days ago... and she told me I might want to talk to you about it.

Robby: Layla! Who the fuck is Maria?

Me: My friend... I met at that group meeting...

Robby: Oh yeah. With the daughter, and curly hair?

Me: That's her.

Robby: Yeah. You two have gotten close lately...

Me: Yeah we have.

Robby: And your just friends?

Me: Totally, and only.

Robby: Okay…

Me: Well my point is…I brought her up, because when I told Maria about that thing in high-school, I realized that it stayed with me, you know? It like, made an impression, and I, well it, it wasn't a good one. Not really. You know?

It got quiet.

Is he still there?

Me: Robby?

Did he hang up on me?

I was sure he had hung up on me.

I was sure I had said too much.

I can't believe he hung up.

Then my phone rang.

Robby?

It was Robby calling me back.

Robby: Hey sorry! The mountains. Call dropped.

Me: Oh.

Robby: But I want to tell you… thank you Layla. Thank you for sharing that. YYou know… we've known each other for eighteen years, so I'm glad that whatever happened to you, or is happening to you… right now… it's allowing you to say something to me, that you've been needing to say for a long time. And… I'm sorry. I know it's eighteen years too late, but for what it's worth, I am sorry. And I love you… it was… well we were just all so stupid, and dumb back then. And I'm sorry you had to say something to me first, for an apology, or acknowledgment. I am.

I wanted to respond to him; what he said was unexpected, and monumental.

Pills.

Get the pills.

The memory itself, and humiliation it came with, was something I had been tethered to for years; and we'd never spoken about it, not until now.

There it goes.

But even so, it was impossible for me to conjure up a real feeling for the potentially, meaningful moment.

I wish I cared more.

Instead, my mind wandered back to texting Rodney.

Get the pills.

Me: Hey Robby... thank you, and I'm sorry I scared you, I really am, but I'm going to try, and get some sleep. I'm feeling like I could sleep so good now, because of what you said. So thank you. It means a lot. Really.

Robby: Layla... you're sure you're okay? You sound off.

Me: I promise I'm okay. I'm just tired, and I'm due for some good sleep. Thank you for what you said. I love you.

Robby: I love you too.

I hope he believes me.

I don't want to upset him.

* *

As soon as I hung up I ambitiously went back to scrolling through my phone for a potential dealer.

Who has OXY?

That'll do.

What Robby had said felt good (even validating), but the good wasn't good enough to derail my suicide mission.

There wasn't anything that could.

I don't think it will hurt.

I started to feel careless again.

This almost feels good.

The feeling of feeling nothing feels freeing.

I feel fearless.

Shit.

While looking for someone to send my request text to, I scrolled right past Selma's name.

Selma.

I stopped scrolling.

I promised.

The jolt of actually seeing Selma's name, shook me out of my isolated tunnel vision, and threw me back into reality.

Selma.

I would be Maria's Selma.

I fell back into my body, and all I could think of was her.

Maria.

I had to call her.

Call Maria.

So I called.

Don't pick up.

But like Maria, she answered right away.

Maria: Layla! I've been texting, and calling you for days!

I was delirious, and spoke with little regard.

Me: I almost did it Maria.

Maria: Did what? Are you okay? You sound strange.

Me: ...it.

Maria: It! Like it?

Me: I...

Maria: Layla where are you? Please... tell me.

I'm so thirsty.

Me: I need water.

Maria: Layla please, where are you?

Me: I'm home.

Help me.

I broke down, and bursted into an uncontrollable cry.

Please help me.

Me: I'm just so fucking tired.

Maria: Layla...

I couldn't stop crying.

It hurts so bad.

Me: Everything is so heavy...all of the time... like all of the time...all the time. And my body... I'm just so tired. I'm so exhausted.

Maria: Layla...

I was fighting through my tears.

Me: ...it hurts, it splits my bones in half, and makes me want to die.

My heart is racing.

Maybe I shouldn't have called her?

Maria: Layla...

I fucked up.

Maria: Layla, take a breath... what are you doing right now?

I really fucked up.

Me: I'm in my bed.

Maria: You have any pills? Be honest. I won't be mad.

Me: No... I was trying to find someone to text... to get...

Maria: You swear you don't?

I wish I did.

Me: Swear.

Maria: Okay... just stay on the phone with me, okay?

I feel my heart getting faster.

Me: ...

Maria: Layla?... Layla!

Me: I'm here...

Maria: Okay...okay. I was just checking.

I can't feel myself breathing.

Why can't I breathe?

Maria: Layla don't hang up... please... okay? I'm coming over right now, with Angie...just stay on the phone with me...please. Please. Okay?

Me: ...

I could hear Maria starting to cry.

She doesn't cry.

Maria: Layla. Please. Just say okay...please...

Me: ....

Maria's cry had become more defined.

Maria: Layla... please just say okay. Please Layla. Please.

Me: ...

I heard Maria grabbing her things in the background.

Maria: Layla please don't hang up!

Me: ...

Don't do this to her Layla.

Maria: Layla.

Me: ...

I could hear Maria fighting back more tears.

Maria: Layla?

Do not Layla.

Do not do this.

Maria: Layla please.

Me: Okay.

I could hear Maria take a large gasp, and then a breath.

Maria: I'm coming.

* *

It took twenty minutes for Maria to drive to me.

Maria: Stay on the phone.

She kept me on the phone with her, the whole time.

Please help.

For those twenty minutes, Maria asked me to breathe, and had me describe, what she called: my calm place.

Okay.

It was something she learned in one of her groups.

Okay.

She told me to imagine a time, and place, where I could remember breathing, and feeling calm.

Help.

It was hard at first. It took at least ten minutes of breathing, and Maria's calming voice, for me to finally remember this one place I had discovered on a canyon hike.

My heart is slowing down.

The canyon itself was beautiful, and open.

My heart is slowing down.

And as I stayed on the phone with Maria, I vividly remembered this corner of the hiking trail (under a large tree), where leaves were falling everywhere.

It was peaceful.

I can feel my shoulders relaxing.

It was so incredibly quiet.

I can hear myself breathe.

It was my calm place.

I can feel myself breathing.

For the remaining ten minutes of Maria's drive, she had me describe my calm place to her, over and over again...

...the shades of brown of the leaves

...the crooked shape of the tree

...the clear sky that day

...the 70 degree humid free temperature

...the calm breeze

Over, and over again until Maria arrived.

Just keep breathing.

Once she got to my place, Maria handed me Angelica, told me to sit down, and went into my kitchen to grab two bowls (which she filled with ice water), and put together Angelica's crib.

What's the ice for?

Then she handed me the bowls.

Maria: Put your hands in there, and breathe.

Me: The ice? Why?

Maria: Layla. Just fucking do it.

Me: Yeah. Okay.

While I sat with my hands in the shockingly cold water, Maria put Angelica down in the travel crib, and explained how the ice, would help bring me back into my body.

I hope it works.

Then Maria walked over to sit by me, laid her head on my lap, and began to cry.

Is she okay?

Maria: Thank you.

Me: For what?

Maria: For not doing it.

She's not mad at me?

Me: You're not mad at me?

The ice is working.

Maria: No I'm not. I'm happy you called.

Maria lifted her head up off my lap, looked at me, and wiped tears from her eyes.

Maria: You are brave... you know. You were ready to jump off the fucking edge. But you didn't, you called, and when you did, that was you fighting for yourself. So I think you're really brave.

I think she's really brave.

I took my hands out of the cold water, wiped them on my shirt, and gave her a giant hug.

Me: I love you.

Maria: I love you, too.

I don't deserve her.

Do I?

* *

I would later discover that Maria never slept that night.

Maria: I wanted to make sure you were safe.

* *

The very next morning, the two of us pulled up to the double glass doors, of an all-glass building.

Kind of like high-school.

A seven-story building dedicated to the rehabilitation of the broken, depressed, and exhausted. An oddly intimidating building, especially made for people like me.

I wish I would've gone with Angie.

Maria dropped Angie off at daycare first, so it was now just her and I in the car... staring at the enormous tower.

Fuck.

Me: I don't know Maria...

I was scared shitless.

Maria: Hey...it's gonna be fine.

She takes my trembling hand.

Maria: You know, I was here before, too.

Me: Here?

She was?

Maria: Yeah here... only I wasn't going to use pills, or a gun. I was going to jump... on the same night I found out I was pregnant. It was like, something came over me, and I just let go...of all of it.

And before I knew it, I was on my balcony, just leaning, and looking. I even got a chair, so I could stand up on it, and just...step off... just like that. And that's the scary part, right? Like...how easy it feels to just let go.

Me: It is.

Maria: Yeah, but when I took that step up onto the chair... no lie... por favor...someone's baby started crying! For real! A fucking baby started crying!... What are the odds right? And then... I don't know, I just stepped down.

Shit.

I realized I had been squeezing Maria's hand tightly.

For a moment we sat quietly, content with the volume of our tears.

Me: But how'd you find this place?

Maria: I didn't. I was brought here, like you... because after I stepped down, I broke down. Hard. Dramatically. And I was really loud, too. I mean I was realizing what had almost happened. And I must have sounded so terrifying, that my neighbor came right over, and knocked on my door to check on me.

Me: The guy who wears rain boots all the time?

Maria giggled.

Maria: No. Not him. My other neighbor. The woman who's husband passed away from covid.

Me: That's right. Fuck.

Maria: Yeah... fuck covid, and all of 2020! But okay... so that night, I told her everything... about my brother, my dad, the baby, the fact that I had almost just jumped... I mean I don't remember most of it... but I know I told her everything...and then... that place...

Maria looked over toward the building.

Maria: This is where she brought me the next day... to her office.

Me: She was your therapist?

Maria: Yep. Dr. Angelica Brown is a therapist there, but she actually brought me into someone else, who she trusted, and thought I'd like. Because, like... she's my neighbor.

Me: Wait Angelica! Like...your Angelica?

Maria: Yes. That woman saved my life... so I absolutely named baby-girl after her.

Me: Oh I had no idea.

Maria: What? That my neighbor saved my life, I named my daughter after her, and I almost killed myself? I mean we've only known each other for a year! I gotta save some of the mystery... and also... it's about you right now. And that's okay. It should be. I'm not swimming in the deep end... you are.

What if this doesn't work?

Me: I'm just scared it won't work.

I'm scared I'm too broken.

Maria: Layla... just give it a chance, and some time. I mean, it took me three years to get to the point where I could even breathe again... to where I could be here, like this, for you, for Angie... for myself. So you just gotta give it time, and a chance... and you gotta take the first step...you gotta go inside.

I took a big inhale.

Me: ...

Maria looked at me, and then gently pulled her hand away from mine, so she could take out the joint she had pre-rolled in the cigarette case (which she had been keeping in her back pocket).

I think I'm too broken.

Maria lit it up, and handed it over to me for the first hit.

Maria: Here...take this before you go in there... then you might calm down enough, and start talking, like how you do when you get stoned with me... then you'll tell her everything! Just like you tell me.

I took the joint from Maria.

Me: But then she's gonna know I'm high.

Maria: Yeah she is! Don't hide it from her either, let her know what she's working with. Let's see if she's as qualified as I know Dr. Angelica is! Plus she talks to people on drugs all the time... I'm sure of it. I bet she probably even prescribed some of them, too!

I laughed.

I still don't want to go.

Maria had made me laugh, but I was still sure I'd have to endure, what I anticipated would be a solid hour of being judged, and humiliated.

But...

But if I didn't go, Maria swore she'd baker-act me, which I understood (I almost did the same thing with Selma).

I wish I had.

The fear of Maria's blunt honesty, and surrendering to seventy-two hours under government watch, had started to over-power my fear of facing myself.

Alright.

Alright!

Fuck it.

Maria: Hey Layla. I love you a lot, and I'm proud of you.

With some lingering fear, and hesitancy, I finally got out of the car.

Me: I love you too.

Then I closed the car door.

Maria: Mira amor... I'm gonna park, and wait in my car, the whole time, right over there.

She pointed to the parking lot across the street.

Pretend you feel safe.

I stopped to ask her one more question.

Me: Will it work?

Maria: What? That? In there?

Maria looked toward the glass building.

Me: Yeah... what if... I'm not... like what if I'm... I mean what if...what if it doesn't...work?

Maria took a breath, and looked down at her perfectly gelled manicured nails, then back up to me.

Maria: "Look, Layla... in there, the more you go in there, and do that, the more you'll able to wrap your head around what the fuck is going on inside that wild, beautiful brain of yours. And I mean, you'll always be you, and have your shit right? But like... for me, I'm not this brand new person, with a new past, or an even a better present! But!... I do feel like I'm steering my own ship now, instead of feeling held hostage in it. And right now... girl... you are being held fucking hostage.

I am.

I tried to take a step.

Take a step Layla.

Maria: You sure you don't want me to walk in there with you? I will.

Me: Kind of.

I desperately do.

Me: But you've done more than enough… for the rest of our lives…you've done enough.

Maria smiled.

I'm safe.

Maria: Well I'm not done.

I finally felt the courage to walk away from the car, and toward the doors. The ones that seemed to be anxiously waiting for me to walk through them.

Shit.

Okay.

You can do this.

I took a breath, another really deep breath, and considered turning around, and running the fuck away.

Selma.

I was tempted to let myself down, but not her.

Maria.

I didn't want to let Maria down. So, in that final moment of decision making, I relied on my love for another, to be motivating enough to help me face the perfectly etched out three way fork in the road. So I stopped one last time, and held my breath, as I took into consideration my three options.

ONE: Keep avoiding the past

Which will inevitably, always be fucked.

TWO: Try embracing the present

Which I'll never experience, if I keep avoiding the past.

THREE: Do neither

And die.

I walked closer to the front doors.

What is going to happen in there?

Then I stopped to check on Maria once more, and forced myself to take another breath.

Come on Layla.

I inhaled deeply.

You can do it!

I focused really hard, and then made myself exhale.

You can fucking do it!

It was the longest exhale, too.

Just one fucking step!

Then I inhaled again.

Don't turn around!

Then finally on that third giant exhale...

Layla, please.

...I took my first step inside.

Here you go.

I'M GETTING MY
CAPTAINS LICENSE

45

Maria: PTSD Layla! Geez! Fuck! The build up! That was almost as bad as the actual night. I mean it's been a minute, but fucking shit! I mean trigger warning next time! I'm not trying to relive that. At all. Fuck!

Me: I'm sorry.

Maria: No sorries Layla! Damage is done.

We laugh, and Maria lights up the joint one last time.

Maria: So you're sleeping here tonight, right?

Me: Yes ma'am. I have therapy next door at Dr. Angies.

Maria: Good. And I put your favorite blanket out for you.

Me: Thank you my love.

Maria: No problem... hey Layla!

Me: Yeah?

Maria: I'm really grateful you're here.

Me: Me too.

I smile with humility, and Maria giggles.

Maria: Hey, so here's something more pleasant to think about while falling asleep, other than your trauma! Lord! So ...I read that orgasms don't always equate to good sex.

Me: Oh no? Then what does?

Maria: Well my therapist suggested to consider a theory that defines fines "good sex" as: giving the body the type of experience that nurtures the nervous system, before, during, and after sex.

Me: Well fuck me.

Maria: Or not.

Me: Ha!

Maria: Yeah well... just marinate on that while you drift off into dreamland, especially after this uplifting trip down memory lane. I mean it's pretty en-par. No?

Me: It definitely is.

She passes me the joint, I take my last hit of the night, and pass it back to Maria.

Me: Thank you for everything Maria... seriously.

Maria: Thank you.

Maria takes her last hit, finally puts it out, and as she heads out to her bedroom, she stops for a moment.

Maria: Hey Layla.

I turn toward her, as I lay my blanket on the couch.

Me: Yeah?

Maria sings out to me.

Maria: Oh boy you know...

I laugh, and sing back to her.

Me: ...you can't escape me!

Then finally, from opposite sides of the room, we sing together in perfectly, imperfect harmony.

Maria and I: Cause you'll always be my...

REBEL

IN

VENUS

If you, or someone you know, is in crisis and in need of immediate help, please contact:

National Sexual Assault Hotline 800-656-4673

National Suicide Prevention Lifeline 988